HANGNAILS

THE MYSTERY OF THE BUTCHERED BANKER

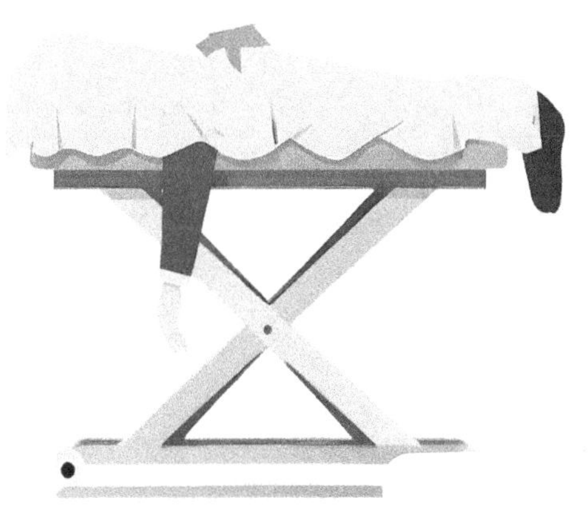

JOAN BRUCE

ISBN: 978-1-962402-23-1

Cover design by Mikey Brooks, mikeybrooks.com

Published by

Fideli Publishing, Inc.
119 W. Morgan St.
Martinsville, IN 46151
www.FideliPublishing.com

In Memory of my Sister
ELIZABETH ANNE REDDICK
1949–2022

CHAPTER 1

"Dammit, Walter, where are you?"

I kept repeating that question to myself as I paced back and forth inside Tips & Toes on Monday night.

Walter A. Morgan III was twenty minutes late for his weekly hangnail treatment. On my day off, no less. I honestly don't know why I put up with him. Walter's more trouble than he's worth.

My weekly meetings with Walter began three months ago. I dropped by his bank after work to refinance the outstanding loan on Bobby's pickup. He's my ex.

During our divorce hearing two years ago, Judge Randall Stone ordered Bobby to hand over his red F-150 truck to me. Truth be told, I wasn't interested in Bobby's vehicle. I just wanted the judge to make Bobby pay to fix my Chevy clunker.

Bobby cried like a baby at the judge's decision. His truck was his pride and joy. He cared more about it than he did me.

But it served him right. Bobby didn't hire an attorney. Said no judge in his right mind would give me anything.

Boy, was he wrong!

Bobby hadn't counted on Judge Stone spending most of his time gawking at my long, slender legs and the black leather miniskirt I wore that day.

But, back to Walter.

Once I sat in his spacious office, he asked if I worked at the nail salon. When I said yes, he wanted to know how much a manicure cost. Talk about confused. I wanted to refinance my truck loan, not discuss manicures. But, I rattled off our salon prices and didn't say another word.

Walter was also quiet. Then, as his eyes slowly moved away from my V-neck sweater, he said he'd drop by next Monday at six o'clock.

"But the salon isn't open on Mondays."

"I know," he replied, giving me a stern look. "You probably have keys to open it, don't you? Just show up, I'll make it worth your while." I figured Walter wasn't used to folks talking back to him.

Bless his heart, Walter did make it worth my while. He handed me a twenty-dollar tip. But as my late Grandma Thompson often used to say, everything comes at a price. And, Walter had a few ground rules for me to follow.

First, I couldn't tell anyone about his hangnails, including Madge Parsons, the owner of Tips & Toes. Second, nobody could be present when he showed up. Not exactly a problem since we're not open then.

"Bartonsville is a very conservative town," Walter explained.

Duh. Like I didn't know that already?

"Practically everyone who lives here is a red-blooded Republican," he continued. "They have certain unwritten rules and expectations. One is not wanting to see their beloved bank president having his nails done. They'd likely get the wrong idea. Might pull their money out of my bank. We can't let that happen, now, can we?"

No sir.

His other rules were right out of a B-level spy novel. The blind on the front door needed to be lowered to signal that the coast was clear. Then, I had to wait until Walter knocked three times before unlocking the door. To tell you the truth, Walter's rules were downright silly, but then again, twenty bucks is twenty bucks.

I showed up at 6:05 p.m. I would have been on time, but the dryers at Sun & Suds were acting up again. Some of my clothes were still damp when I pulled them out of the dryer.

It didn't matter. Walter hadn't arrived. That was odd. He's always on time. While I waited, I decided to freshen up. No sense looking frumpy for my best tipper. I pulled out my banana clip and let my blonde hair fall to my shoulders. I then grabbed the hairbrush in my handbag.

"Not bad," I said, admiring myself in the large mirror behind our front counter. "A lift here, little tuck there and you'd be one hot momma, Candi."

I checked my Betty Boop watch. Five minutes had passed. Walter still hadn't shown up. Where was he?

On a recent visit, Walter had given me his cell phone number. I dug my phone out of the bottom of my handbag and dialed his number. The phone rang four or five times before going to voicemail. "Hey, Walter. It's Candi. I'm waiting for you."

After putting my phone away, I glanced at the front door. The blind was up. Darn, how had I forgotten our signal? I rushed over and lowered the blind. Now Walter should be here any minute. I sat down on a hard, plastic chair in our reception area and picked up the newest issue of *People* magazine. Might as well get caught up on the latest celebrity gossip while I waited.

After reading all about Taylor Swift's latest boyfriend, I glanced at my watch again. 6:32 p.m. Darn him. Walter was a no show. I called his cell once more, but he didn't answer.

I stood up, shut off the lights, picked up my handbag, and grabbed my new rabbit fur jacket off the coat rack beside the front door. I bought it last week at a warehouse liquidation sale in Indianapolis. Forty dollars marked down from one fifty. What a steal! I locked the front door and stepped outside. The town square was deserted except for my truck.

As I stood there in the crisp October air, I wondered if Walter was working late and that's why he hadn't answered my calls. Maybe I should check on him. If he's still in his office, I could take care of his hangnails while he continued to sign papers or whatever a bank president does. I always carry a portable nail kit in my handbag for such emergencies.

To be honest, I could use Walter's tip this week. I'm already short of cash. Bought too many fall decorations at Walmart over the weekend. I can't resist their two-for-one specials.

Madge doesn't pay us until Friday. My heart also has been set all day on stopping by the Grab & Run convenience store on my way home and treating myself to a package of Ho Hos. A chocolate fix is a great way to end a day.

Instead of driving to the bank, I decided to walk. The cool air would help to calm me after being stood up by Walter. Besides, I felt nice and toasty in my new rabbit fur jacket.

As I strutted across the sidewalk next to the Barton County Courthouse, I spotted a lawn sign for the town's annual Foliage Festival. It starts Thursday night. When I was seventeen, I was first runner-up in the festival's talent contest. I would have won if the batteries in my hand mic hadn't died while I sang "Stand by Your Man." It made me so mad. I definitely was more talented than Cindy Campbell and her twirling batons. By the way, when did throwing a pair of metal sticks in the air become a talent?

Once at the end of the courthouse sidewalk, I crossed the street and stood in front of the State Bank of Bartonsville. The two-story limestone structure is the tallest building in town. As I peeked through the bank's plate glass front door, I spotted a light on beyond the lobby, but nobody was moving around.

Hmmm?

Should I pound on the door? No, I finally decided. It might set off a silent burglar alarm and bring the cops running. I didn't need that hassle tonight. So I walked around the corner of the building and peeked through a side window. Still no sign of life. Since I'd come this far, I figured I might as well check out the rear of the bank.

I stepped into the alley. The back door was slightly ajar. That was odd. Maybe someone was robbing the bank. Was that why Walter missed his appointment and didn't answer my calls? The poor man was tied up in his office.

I knew one thing. I wasn't hanging around to find out what happened next. I'm too young to die. As I got ready to leave, I didn't see any getaway car idling in the alley.

Hmmm?

Maybe the heist was over, and the robbers simply forgot to close the back door. This is Bartonsville after all. We probably don't have the brightest bank robbers living here.

If the bank wasn't robbed, then maybe Walter had heard my voice mail message and simply left the back door unlocked for me. I decided to step inside. The bank's narrow hallway was dark and creepy. It reminded me of those scary movies I watch on TV late at night when I can't sleep.

I carefully removed my five-inch stilettos before tiptoeing down the tiled floor. No sense having some weirdo hear me and jump out from behind a closed door with a razor-sharp hatchet in his hand. From previous visits, I knew Walter's office was near the front lobby. When I reached it, his door was open a crack. Maybe he was expecting me.

"I'm here," I said after putting my shoes back on, pushing the door wide open, and walking inside. I didn't want to embarrass Walter if he was having a quick cat nap.

Walter was sitting in his big black leather chair, dressed in a gray banker's suit. Both of his arms were resting comfortably on top of his large oak desk. He looked ready for his hangnail treatment.

"Give me a minute to get set up, Walter," I said, moving across his hardwood floor to the side of his desk.

He didn't respond.

I tossed my fur jacket on a matching black leather chair in front of Walter's desk before rummaging through my handbag.

"Where's my darn manicure set?" I asked myself as I bent over to take a closer look inside my handbag.

"There you are," I said, pulling it from my bag.

As I stood, I tripped on the edge of the plush Oriental carpet underneath Walter's desk and fell forward. I tried to catch myself, but ended up brushing against Walter's chair anyway.

He responded by falling face first on his desk. A large hunting knife was sticking out of his back. Walter was dead.

"Omigod," I screamed.

I screamed again as my eyes remained fixated on the shiny silver blade. Who'd want to stab poor Walter? And, with such a big, sharp knife?

As I stepped back, I happened to glance down at his hands.

"Why are you wearing pink nail polish?"

This was all too weird for me. Time to leave. As I slowly backed away from Walter's desk, a voice behind me shouted, "Freeze!"

CHAPTER 2

Omigod, my heart was pounding so loud I thought it would fly out of my mouth and land on Walter's expensive Oriental rug. Who was behind me? The killer?

Clutching my bosom, I slowly turned to see who had snuck up on me. And there they were. Nathan Sloan and Frank Turner of the Bartonsville Police Department. Their big black pistols were pointed directly at my girls.

Some older town folks call the pair Mutt and Jeff. Nate is the short, round one; Frank is tall and thin.

"Come on, boys," I said, slowly raising my arms in the air. "Put your pistols away. I'm not packin.'"

"What are you doing here, Candi?" Frank barked. His gun was still pointed at me.

"Me? I should be asking you that question," I said, glaring at him. "You and Nate sneaking up on me? You scared the bejesus out of me. I could have had a heart attack. Why didn't you sound your police siren first? And, there's no need to shout. I have perfect hearing."

Frank shrugged and looked at his partner.

"So, Candi, what are you doing here?" Nate asked.

"What's it look like?" I replied. "I needed to make a bank withdrawal, but I forgot my ATM card."

Nate didn't say anything. He was never too quick with comebacks, even in high school.

Meanwhile, Frank wandered over to take a closer look at Walter.

"Mister Morgan's dead," he declared after turning back to me and Nate.

"Congratulations," I said, planting both hands on my hips. "That's some mighty fine police work on your part, Frank."

"Shut up, Candi," he snapped. "Did you stab Mister Morgan?"

"Yeah, my nail file was too dull, so I used my trusty hunting knife instead."

"This is no laughing matter."

"I know. I'm trying not to cry."

Frank ignored my remark and asked, "Why did you paint his fingernails pink?"

"Frank Turner," I said, stepping off the edge of Walter's Oriental rug and stomping my feet on his hardwood floor for added emphasis. "I can't believe you asked me that question.

I'm a professional manicurist. I'd never paint a client's nails that way. Madge Parsons would fire me in a heartbeat. Besides, why would Walter choose pink-colored nail polish? It doesn't match his complexion."

Frank shrugged and left the office.

"You shouldn't tease Frank," Nate said as he moved closer. "He takes everything so seriously. Now, what are you *really* doing here, Candi?"

I looked straight at Nate. He has big, beautiful brown cow eyes. Eyes that can melt a girl's heart quicker than a bowl of chocolate swirl ice cream on a hot summer night. At first, I didn't know what to say. Should I lie or tell him the truth?

"It's like this, Nate," I began. "I'm thinking of opening my own nail salon and I wanted to know if Walter might loan me some money."

"What have you got against working for Madge? She's one of my mom's best friends."

Great. Let's hope this conversation doesn't get back to Madge, or I'll be looking for a new job.

"I found Walter this way when I walked in the back door. Why would I murder him if he might loan me some money?"

Nate nodded.

I had overcome his big brown cow eyes. He was buying my fib.

"That doesn't explain the pink nail polish."

"Nate, like I told Frank, I'd never paint a client's nails that way. Walter either did it himself or someone else did it for him."

"Why would Walter agree to that?" Nate asked.

"You tell me," I said. "Everyone in town thinks he's a little different. Maybe Walter had some secrets he didn't want the rest of us to know about. Besides, with a knife sticking out of his back, he really didn't have a choice."

"That may be," Frank said as he re-entered Walter's office. "But it doesn't look good for you, Candi. Me and Nate finding you here. You'll have some real explaining to do if you plan to talk yourself out of this situation."

Frank was right. Things weren't looking good for me.

"But I didn't do anything," I said, pleading my case. "Why would I murder Walter? There are lots of other people I'd rather kill first. My ex-husband, Bobby DeCarlo, for one. Besides, I don't carry around a large hunting knife in my handbag to stab people on a whim. The only weapon I carry is a can of mace."

"That's enough about killing people." Frank said, shooting me a dirty look. "We need to be more respectful of Mister Morgan's soul."

Walter's soul? Has Frank suddenly found religion?

"Where were you?" Nate asked Frank.

"In the alley calling the station," Frank replied. "The cell reception is better out there. I talked to Mary."

Frank was talking about Mary Donovan. She's the police department's night dispatcher and the smartest woman I know. She's also one of my clients.

"Mary called the new chief to tell him what's happened. She wants one of us to bring Candi to the station for more questioning. The other one can stay here and guard Mister Morgan's body until the Chief and coroner arrive."

Nate and Frank grinned at each other before playing a game of rock, paper, scissors. Frank lost. Nate said he'd drive me to the police station. He reached behind his belt for his handcuffs.

"Do I have to wear them?" I said in my best whiney voice.

"Yes," Frank replied. "Right now, you're the prime suspect in this murder investigation. You have to wear the cuffs. Now, Nate put them on her."

Nate had me turn around so he could cuff me.

"Are they too tight?" he asked.

"No, you did a fine job," I replied. "Now, do me a favor and throw my coat over my shoulders. This way, if we run into anyone outside, they won't see my new bracelets."

A minute later, Nate and I left the bank through the back door. The sun had set, but a floodlight in the alley cast enough light for us to safely make our way to Nate's shiny black and white squad car.

"Hey, guys, what's going on?"

I looked up. Johnny Edwards was taking in the whole humiliating scene in his motorized wheelchair.

Like my ex-husband, Johnny had been a star athlete at Bartonsville High School before joining the Army after graduation. A year and a half later, Johnny came home from Afghanistan minus a leg and several fingers. A roadside land mine had blown up in front of him. Johnny now spends his days tooling around town in his motorized wheelchair, getting into everyone's business.

"Come on, guys, you can tell me what happened," he pleaded. "Nate, did you catch Candi red-handed trying to rob Walter's bank?"

"Mind your own business, Johnny," I said, glaring at him.

Nate also chimed in. "It's nothing like that Johnny. Just go about your business."

Johnny didn't move as Nate unlocked his squad car and guided me into the back seat before we sped off. I was grateful Nate didn't turn on his siren. No sense letting everyone in town know I was now the guest of honor in his cruiser.

I was still fuming over our run-in with Johnny when I looked up and noticed Nate staring at me in his rear-view mirror.

"What's the matter, Nate?"

"I'm worried, Candi," he said softly. "That situation back at the bank. You, Walter, and that big hunting knife. It doesn't look good for you."

"I know, but you gotta believe me. I'm innocent. Why would I kill poor Walter? He was such a nice man."

Nate nodded before changing the subject. "I ran into Mandy the other day."

Mandy Malone is my best friend in the whole world. We've been besties since our first day of kindergarten at the Dwight D. Eisenhower Elementary School. We've both survived loser husbands and are struggling to make our way in a man's world. We're like blood sisters and call each other practically every day.

"What was she doing?" I asked, anxious to talk about something other than Walter Morgan.

"Speeding on the west side of town," Nate replied. "I had to pull her over."

"How fast was she going?"

"Fifty in a thirty."

"Did you write her a ticket? Or handcuff her and haul her off to jail?"

"No, I simply warned Mandy to keep her fancy Jaguar convertible within the speed limits."

"Still have a crush on her, don't you, Nate?"

"Why would you say that?"

Poor Nate. He stalked Mandy in high school like most of the other boys. Only Nate was shy, so instead of talking to Mandy, he'd leave notes on her desk. Sometimes, he'd steal flowers out of a neighbor's yard and leave them at the foot of her locker. I once asked Mandy why she wouldn't go out with him.

"Who wants to date the boy next door type?" she replied. "Give me a bad boy any day."

And, that's how Mandy ended up marrying her first husband, Butch Muldoon, and became a biker momma.

It was another minute or two before Nate pulled his squad car into the side entrance to the police station. He helped me out of the back seat and then steered me through the station's side door. Once inside, we climbed three steps to a tiled landing. Sitting behind the plexiglass window in front of us was Mary Donovan.

Mary has worked at the police department for as long as I can remember. She's not much taller than Nate, but don't be fooled by her tiny stature or her short, close-cropped white hair. Mary is one tough cookie. Rumor has it she knocked heads with more than one local yokel in her day and won.

"Well… look who's here," Mary said through the tiny opening in her plexiglass window. "If it isn't the always fashionably attired, Candi DeCarlo. What crime against the good citizens of Bartonsville have you committed tonight?"

"Thanks for the compliment, Mary," I said, ignoring her snide remark. "I'm glad you like my new jacket. I picked it up at a warehouse liquidation sale last week in Indianapolis. It was a real steal."

"A real steal, huh?" Mary said, leaning closer to her window's opening. "Do we need to arrest you for that, too?"

Mary and Nate laughed hysterically.

"Relax, Candi," Mary said after a minute. "Frank called and told me what happened at the bank. Tell me it ain't so. You didn't stab Walter Morgan, did you?"

"Mary, how can you ask such a thing?" I replied. "You know me. I wouldn't harm a flea. Have you forgotten how gentle I am when I paint your nails? I was simply dropping off our night deposit."

"But, sweetie, the last time I checked the night deposit window was on the outside corner of the bank. What were you doing in Walter's office?"

No wonder everybody in town thinks Mary should be the police chief. She's too darn smart for her own good. She put me in an awkward spot. I faked a cough, trying to buy a little more time to come up with a better excuse for being inside Walters' office. I didn't want to tell her the truth. After all, treating Walter's hangnails was supposed to be top secret.

"Well, it's like this," I said, trying to avoid looking directly at her. "Walter called me earlier today. Said he wanted to do something nice for his wife's birthday next week. So, he had me drop by the bank after work to explain our services. He wanted to give her a gift certificate to the salon."

"That was so thoughtful of him," Mary said when I finished telling her my little white lie. "I've met Mrs. Morgan. The good Lord wasn't particularly kind to her in the looks department. Who knows, maybe you could have worked some of your magic on the poor thing. Now, we'll never know. By the way, isn't Tips & Toes closed on Mondays?"

Darn, Mary's good.

She then gave me one of her patented smirks before reaching down and pressing a buzzer to unlock the door. Nate grabbed my arm and carefully steered me through the doorway.

"Put her in an interrogation room, Nate. The new chief should be calling any minute. He's probably still at the bank, but he'll want to interrogate Candi himself. Here's a magazine for her to read."

"Thanks, Mary," I replied. "Do me a favor? Call Mandy and let her know I'm here."

"Okay, but I have another question. Are we still on for Wednesday? My appointment is at half past three."

"Sure thing. If I'm not still in jail."

CHAPTER 3

Once inside the tiny interrogation room, Nate had me sit on a rickety wooden chair behind a beat-up gray metal table. This furniture was worse than anything I'd ever found at garage sales or the Goodwill store. Nate tossed Mary's magazine on the table and told me to stay put. He was taking his dinner break.

And judging by Nate's waistline, I'd say he was headed to Ralph's Diner for the Monday night special. It's a giant tenderloin on a toasted sesame seed bun, a large order of fries, a side of cole slaw, and a medium drink. It could satisfy Paul Bunyan's appetite and it's only eight dollars and seventy-nine cents—sales tax and tip not included.

"Want anything from the diner?" Nate asked.

"No, I don't plan to be here much longer," I said. "But say hi to Ritchie if he's still there."

Ritchie Southerland owns Ralph's Diner. Why the diner isn't called Ritchie's is a long story, better left for another day.

I worked there for nearly twenty years before I saved enough money to attend beauty college in Indianapolis and become a professional manicurist.

After Nate left, I picked up Mary's magazine hoping it was the same *People* magazine I had been reading at the nail salon. I wanted to reread the article about Taylor Swift's latest boyfriend. Was he really a professional football player?

One look at the cover dashed any hope of that. *Soldier of Fortune?*

Why's Mary reading this stuff? I know she thinks of herself as one tough cookie. And, she would have made a darn good cop if the old farts on the town council had given her the chance. They didn't think Bartonsville was ready for a female cop when she was first hired. Still don't. But, *Soldier of Fortune? Really?*

Maybe Mary plans to retire soon and become a mercenary in some third-world country. I can see her now. Jumping out of a plane in the middle of an overgrown jungle with an AK-47 clutched in her hands and two belts of ammo strapped across her chest.

Whew. I need to turn off my TV at night. I watch too many Steven Seagal movies. I was starting to scare myself. I know one thing, though. Mary will have some explaining to do when she has her nails done this Wednesday.

I glanced at my Betty Boop watch. 7:55 p.m. When was this new police chief going to show up? Halloween? It had already been an hour since I found Walter's body. How long did it take someone to stare at a dead guy? Especially when the cause of death was plainly homicide. But, if this new chief was anything like any of the previous chiefs, he was probably still finding his way back to the station.

I began tapping my new, fire-engine red acrylics on the metal table. Carefully, I might add. Madge Parsons applied them last week. She's still the best manicurist around even if she now spends most of her day perched on a wooden stool behind our front counter, watching her soaps on a tiny portable pink TV and collecting clients' money.

I looked up when I heard someone unlock the door. Nate must be back from the diner. Can you believe him? He locked me in before he left. And, after I promised not to go anywhere. What if I had to go potty?

"I figured you'd be thirsty by now, so I brought you a medium Diet Dr. Pepper," Nate said as he stepped into the room. "That's still your drink, right?"

I grabbed the Styrofoam cup from Nate's hand and took a giant swig. Sitting in this interrogation room had made me thirsty. I wanted to yell at him for locking the door, but why bother. Thankfully, I didn't have a restroom emergency.

Besides, Nate was probably following some dumb police procedure.

"Looks like you left some of your dinner on yourself," I said, noticing a big yellow blotch on Nate's blue shirt. "Got a handkerchief?"

"Sure," he said, pulling one out of his back pocket. And a clean handkerchief, I might add. I was duly impressed.

"Looks like mustard," I said, grabbing the handkerchief out of Nate's hand. "Let's see if I can wipe it off for you."

As I began removing the spot, the door to the interrogation room swung open and in walked the most gorgeous guy I'd seen in Bartonsville in a very, very long time.

"Am I interrupting anything?" he asked, flashing a big toothy grin.

Mister Gorgeous was well over six feet tall and had a very trim body. Very trim, indeed. His eyes were dark brown like Nate's and his hair was jet-black with a slight touch of gray at the temples. He had a square jaw and a faint five o'clock shadow. Mister Gorgeous was wearing a white button-down dress shirt, open at the collar, and a pair of black casual slacks. He looked like he'd stepped off the set of one of Madge's soap operas. He couldn't be the new police chief, could he? Why hadn't I met him until now?

"Oh, hi, Chief," Nate said. "Candi's helping me wipe some mustard off my uniform. I had a little accident while on dinner break. Sorry about that."

"That's okay," the Chief said, looking directly at me. "So, you must be Candice DeCarlo."

"That's me," I replied, my mouth still hanging open. "Candice is actually my Christian name. Only I don't think my Mom ever had me baptized. We didn't go to church very often. Mom was usually too tired to get me and my half-brother, Randy, ready for Sunday school, especially after she spent a Saturday night on the town with one of her boyfriends. Anyway, my friends all call me Candi. You can, too."

I couldn't believe myself. I was blathering like a love-sick schoolgirl with a crush on her handsome high school English teacher. Get a grip, Candi. You're forty-two years old with a twenty-five-year-old daughter and two grandbabies. Women your age aren't supposed to act that way. Then again, when did I ever do what I was supposed to do?

"Okay, Candi. That's what I'll call you. I'm Chief Dan Cobb. But, you can call me Dan if you'd like," he said, sticking out his right hand to shake mine. "It's nice to meet you."

Dan had a big, warm hand. I wanted to grab it and hold it next to my bosom. But, he probably wouldn't believe me if I told him I was simply showing him some Hoosier hospitality.

"Have a seat, Candi," he said. "I'm sorry it took me so long at the bank. I was waiting on the state police investigators to arrive and give me a preliminary assessment of the situation. This shouldn't take too long."

Take all night, Dan. In fact, if you want to drop by my place later, and ask me some more probing questions in private, I'm fine with that, too.

Dan sat across from me. He then spoke to Nate who was still rubbing the last of the mustard off his shirt.

"Check with Frank to see if the coroner has shown up at the bank. Mary was sending someone to Walter Morgan's house to tell his wife what happened. See how that went."

"Yessir," Nate said, as he left the interrogation room.

"Now, Candi," Dan said, looking straight at me. "Why don't you tell me what you were doing inside Mister Morgan's bank tonight?"

I like a man who gets right to the point. As he waited for my answer, Dan's eyes locked on mine. All I wanted to do was crawl underneath the table and hide from his intense stare.

"Like I told Mary," I said, clicking my nails on the metal table. "Walter invited me to the bank to talk about buying his wife a gift certificate for her birthday."

"Are you absolutely sure that's what happened?"

Dan's piercing eyes continued to probe mine for what seemed like an eternity. Finally, he spoke.

"I know it's not easy to talk about what happened tonight, but you can tell me the truth," he said, before laying both of his hands down on the table next to mine. That did it.

"Okay," I said, wilting under his harsh interrogation technique. "I went to the bank to treat Walter's hangnails. I've been taking care of them for the past three months. But Walter was already dead when I walked into his office."

"Good, Candi," Dan said, slapping his hands on the table. "I figured it was something like that. Don't you feel better for having told me the truth?"

I shrugged.

"Why didn't Walter come to your nail salon?" Dan asked. "Wouldn't that have been easier?"

"He usually did, but when he didn't show up tonight, I went looking for him."

"What about the pink nail polish on his nails?"

"Like I told Mary and the guys, I didn't paint Walter's nails pink. It was a very unprofessional job. Besides, his nails were painted with Essie #422."

"What's that?"

"It's a popular brand of nail polish," I said. "But we don't carry Essie products at Tips & Toes. We use only OPI products."

"That's interesting," Dan said, rubbing his chin. "What about the back door? Did you know Mister Morgan was leaving it open for you?"

"No, it was a big surprise to me when I found it open."

Dan jotted down another note in his notebook.

"Can I ask you a question, Dan?"

"Sure."

"Am I under arrest?"

"I can't verify your story right now, so I won't hold you in custody tonight. Besides, our holding cells are being renovated this week. Mary and the guys have vouched for you. Said you're a regular, stay-at-home kind of gal. But if I learn later that you lied to me, I'll arrest you for trespassing on bank property after hours. Until I know who stabbed Mister Morgan, I'll treat you as a person of interest."

"Is there anything else?"

Dan looked up at Nate, who had re-entered the room. "Did Candi have any incriminating evidence on her?"

"No sir. Inside her handbag were some keys, a pink cell phone, a tube of lipstick, a hairbrush, a tiny pouch with a bunch of fingernail equipment, a can of mace, and a few tissues. She didn't have any money."

"Thanks, Nate," he said before turning to me. "One of your girlfriends is waiting for you in the parking lot. She'll drive you home. But promise me you won't leave town until I sort everything out."

I raised my right hand. "I promise."

"Okay, then, you're free to go."

I stood up. My knees were quivering. I couldn't tell if it was from sitting so long on that hard, wooden chair, or if I was suffering from a fatal attraction. I shook the chief's big warm hand again and left.

Mandy was leaning against the hood of her shiny black Jaguar convertible when I walked out of the police station. She was wearing an expensive-looking pink exercise outfit that she probably bought on her last trip to the Fashion Mall in Indianapolis. Her shoulder length black hair was tied up in a ponytail sticking through her pink Colts ball cap. She was also puffing on a menthol cigarette.

For years, I've yelled at Mandy to stop smoking, but she doesn't listen. When she spotted me, Mandy tossed the cigarette on the ground and crushed it with the heel of her pink cowboy boot.

"What's up?" she asked. "You look like hell."

"I think I'm in love."

CHAPTER 4

We jumped into Mandy's Jaguar, fastened our seat belts, and sped off. Once we'd driven a block or so, Mandy asked, "Where'd you get that jacket?"

"Don't you just love it?" I said, sticking my left arm underneath her nose. "I bought it last week in Indianapolis. Got it for next to nothing. Did I get a bargain, or what?"

Mandy turned her attention back to the road. "It's … different."

"You don't like it? What's wrong with it?"

"It makes you look cheap. Like a floozie who hangs out on street corners. If you wanted a real fur coat, I would have loaned you the money. By the way, what's it made of? Muskrat?"

"No, it's rabbit," I said, defending my jacket. "Several bunnies gave up their young lives in the making of this coat. That bothered me at first until I saw the price tag. I don't care what you think. I love my new jacket, and I plan to keep wearing it. But, thanks for offering to loan me the money. However, you know how I am about handouts. I've been getting along on my own since divorcing Bobby."

"I know, sweetie, but you did everything on your own when you were married, too," Mandy said, reaching across and patting the arm of my coat. "I didn't mean to upset you. But you shouldn't wear a miniskirt with that jacket. It gives off the wrong vibe. Wear slacks or long dresses instead."

I was still smarting from Mandy's fashion critique, but, fortunately, she changed the subject.

"What was going on back at the police station? Mary Donovan said the cops found you inside Walter Morgan's office, but she didn't tell me why. You weren't having an affair with him, were you?"

"Mandy Malone!" I said, screaming at her. "It's bad enough that you don't like my new jacket, but now you're accusing me of dating an older man. It just so happens I found Walter sitting in his office with a hunting knife sticking out of the middle of his back."

"What?" Mandy slammed on her brakes before steering her car safely to the side of the road and throwing it into park. "You found Walter murdered inside his bank?"

"Yup."

"So, if you weren't having an affair with him, what were you doing there?"

"I guess I can tell you now that Walter is dead. There's no reason to keep his secret anymore. For the past three months, I've been treating Walter's hangnail problem on Monday nights. Walter missed his appointment tonight, so I went looking for him."

"Walter had hangnails?" Mandy said, pounding the steering wheel with her hand. "Darn. Why didn't you tell me? I thought we were blood sisters and didn't have any secrets between us."

"Don't take this the wrong way, Mandy. Telling you anything is like plastering it on a giant billboard next to the interstate. Besides, Walter made me promise. I couldn't tell anyone. Not even Madge. He said people might get the wrong idea if they found out. I didn't want to lose him as a client. He was a big tipper."

"Wow, I still can't believe it," Mandy said, smacking her steering wheel again. "So, you went over to the bank looking for him, and…."

"His back door was open, so I walked inside and…"

"That's when you found him with the knife in his back?"

"Pretty much, but there's something else I haven't told you. And, you're not going to believe it."

"So, tell me already."

"Walter was wearing Essie #422."

"What? You're kidding me. I use Essie products."

"I'm not kidding. I saw it with my own two eyes. And, guess what else? It was a lousy nail job. He must have tried doing it himself."

"Why would Walter paint his nails pink? Boy, I wish I'd known about this little fetish of his a week ago."

"What are you talking about?"

"I dropped by his bank to extend my credit line. I need to purchase more inventory before the weather gets any worse. As usual, Walter gave me a hard time. He didn't believe a woman could run a chain of discount tire stores. Anyway, if I'd known about his painted nail fetish, I would have found a way to bring it up in our conversation and watch him squirm like a mouse caught in a hawk's talons."

"You would have embarrassed him like that?" I said.

"Sweetie don't be so naïve," Mandy replied. "It's only business. I needed more credit. Walter was a miser. In the business world, you need to use every advantage you can find."

"That's why I don't own a business." I changed the subject. "By the way, thanks for picking me up. I didn't know who else to call."

"No problem," Mandy replied. "So, what did you tell the cops?"

"At first, I said Walter invited me to the bank to talk about buying his wife a gift certificate to the salon."

"Why'd you tell them that?"

"I don't know. I was nervous and didn't want to tell them the truth. You know, about Walter's hangnails. It was a secret."

"But Walter's dead. Once you die, you don't have any more secrets."

"I know, but I wasn't thinking straight."

"Did you finally tell them the truth?"

"Yeah, after Chief Dan Cobb showed up. One look at his dark brown eyes and I melted quicker than butter on a hot cob of corn at the county fair. Have you met him yet? He's gorgeous."

"Dan's handsome," Mandy replied. "I'll give you that. He stopped by the store last week to introduce himself and to check on our security system. It rings into the station if there's a break-in. He seemed all business to me."

"Handsome? Is that all you have to say? I remember a time when bumping into a guy like Dan would have sent you into a swoon. Being a widow certainly has changed you."

"I guess so," Mandy said as she steered her Jaguar back onto the road. "It's still hard getting over the loss of Marvin. He was such a wonderful husband and good provider."

I'll say. When Marvin Malone died two years ago, he left Mandy a five-bedroom house on the far edge of town, a small chain of discount tire stores in southern Indiana and Todd, her stepson, who's only five years younger than her.

"By the way, how are you getting along with Todd these days?" I asked.

"He's still difficult at times, but I've learned how to manage him."

"How so?"

"I call Brenda, his wife. She must say something to him when he comes home from work because the next day, he's like honey dripping off a warm biscuit. Brenda and I have become fast friends. But not like you and me. We're blood sisters. That's why I jumped out of a warm bubble bath tonight and drove straight to the police station."

"It's nice to know our friendship means that much to you. But I need your opinion about something. Think Dan will throw me in jail if he decides I murdered Walter? Right now, he considers me a person of interest. And, you know how I feel about orange jumpsuits. I hate that color. It makes me look fat and washed out."

"Don't worry. If Dan arrests you, I'll talk to Judge Stone. Randall was Marvin's best friend growing up and his college roommate at Indiana University. I won't let him send you to prison."

I wasn't sure if Mandy was handing me a line of bull poopy or if she truly meant what she said. After she married Marvin six years ago, Mandy began hanging out with a different set of folks in town. The Bartonsville Country Club crowd. And even though Marvin has moved on to that big tire store in the sky, Mandy still holds sway over these people. Maybe she has pictures of them from her days as the country club's dining room hostess. I mean, who knows what goes on at an exclusive place like that? They can't play golf all day. I crossed my fingers and hoped to never find out.

"So, what was it like staring at old Walter?" Mandy asked, bringing the conversation back to him.

"Creepy. He was slumped over his desk with the knife sticking out of his back."

A minute later, Mandy drove her car onto the town square. My truck was the only vehicle left on the street.

"I'm driving up to the Fashion Mall this weekend," Mandy said. "Want to come?"

"I don't know. I usually clean my place on Sunday afternoons."

"Sorry, I forgot. You don't have a housekeeper, do you?"

"We can't all be rich like you, Mandy."

"I guess not," she said, a huge smile forming on her face. "Well, if you change your mind, call me on my cell."

With that, Mandy and I blew air kisses at each other before I climbed out of her car. She laid a stretch of rubber as she pulled away. I guess you can do that if you own your own tire store. Or, perhaps Mandy was hoping some bubbles were still left in her tub.

I climbed into my truck and glanced at my watch. Luckily, Betty Boop glows in the dark. 9:35 p.m. All I wanted to do was drive home, jump into my nice warm bed, hug Freddy, my teddy bear. It's not every night you find a dead body, get interrogated by the police, and told you're a person of interest in a homicide investigation!

CHAPTER 5

"Want your usual?" Joanie Sullivan asked as I plopped down on one of the stools at Ralph's Diner on Tuesday morning.

I nodded. Joanie is barely taller than the top of the lunch counter. She has beautiful gray hair and owns many pairs of Nike sneakers. Michael Jordan would be envious. Joanie started working at Ralph's long before I did. And, I waitressed there for nearly twenty years.

"What's with the farmers?" I asked as I nodded in the direction of a group of men in bib overalls and John Deere ballcaps. They were huddled around the big oak table near the front door.

"Why are you asking?"

"When I walked in a minute ago, they all stopped yammering and began staring at me. It was creepy. They've seen me in this outfit before. Is anything sticking out?"

"Nothing more than usual," Joanie replied. "They've probably never before seen a murder suspect dressed in a miniskirt and a tight sweater."

"Huh?"

"Haven't you seen this morning's paper?"

"No. I don't like newspapers. Who wants to read about people shooting each other all the time? Not me. The news is too depressing."

"I should have known," Joanie said, grabbing a coffee pot off the back counter. "I'll be back in a second."

Joanie marched over to the farmers' table. As she poured refills, she snatched a paper out of the hands of one of them.

"Here you go," Joanie said, tossing the paper at me. "You made the front page."

While Joanie wandered off to retrieve my cinnamon swirl and medium Diet Dr. Pepper, I picked up the *Barton County Beacon,* the county's only daily newspaper. The large black headline across the front page read: "Walter Morgan Dead in Bank; Woman Questioned."

J. Michael McPherson, the *Beacon's* senior reporter, wrote the story. I've never liked him. When I worked at the diner, he'd waltz in every day as the clock struck twelve, acting like some big shot, his chest puffed up and his gut sticking out over a pair of wrinkled khaki pants. Rumor has it that he's looking for that one big story to get himself a better job in Indianapolis or Chicago. This better not be it.

I quickly read his story. Darn, Joanie was right. McPherson made it sound like I was the prime suspect in Walter's death. No wonder the farmers were gawking. I would, too. I've never met a murder suspect in a miniskirt either.

I picked up the paper and re-read the paragraph that mentioned me.

> Police Chief Dan Cobb confirmed late last night that two of his officers found a woman inside Morgan's office when they arrived at the bank. The Beacon has learned from an anonymous source that the woman was Candi DeCarlo, age unknown, of Bartonsville. When asked what Ms. DeCarlo was doing inside the bank, Chief Cobb refused to acknowledge her identity, but under intense questioning from this reporter, he admitted that the woman remained a 'person of interest' for the time being.

I was still fuming at McPherson's story when I heard a voice to my right say, "How you doin' this morning, beautiful?"

Who was the sweet talker? Hopefully not one of those farmers suddenly feeling frisky. Instead, Ritchie Southerland was standing next to me. I quickly stood up and gave him a huge hug.

Ritchie is still a good-looking man for a guy in his late fifties. He has a slight build, short salt-and-pepper hair, and a neatly trimmed mustache of the same color. He's like the daddy I never had. Well, maybe not exactly. More like a favorite uncle or a slightly older brother. In any case, Ritchie moved to Bartonsville ten years ago after buying the diner from Ralph Simms.

It didn't take Ritchie too long to realize that being gay didn't go over too well in Bartonsville. It's a God-fearing town, after all, and folks here don't think too much of people of different persuasions. So, Ritchie, hoping to gain their goodwill, told everyone Ralph was his long-lost uncle.

Ralph had owned the diner for thirty years before he and Marilyn bought a retirement condo in Florida. He'd been quite popular with the locals. At first, the regulars weren't buying Ritchie's story. Nobody remembered Ralph ever mentioning he had a sister. But once Ritchie began making his cinnamon swirls, nobody cared about his sexual orientation. Their only concern was whether any swirls would still be left when they showed up for their morning Joe.

"What have you done now?" Ritchie asked, as he followed me to the empty booth near the back door.

"Ritchie, you gotta believe me, I didn't do it," I said, as I scooted into the booth. "I didn't have anything to do with Walter Morgan's murder."

"What are you talking about?"

Apparently, Ritchie doesn't read the local paper either. So, I quickly filled him in on Walter's after-hour hangnail treatments and how I'd gone to the bank last night looking for him.

Ritchie's the best confessor I know. He knows how to keep a secret. Mandy, bless her heart, forgets to keep secrets a secret. Anyway, when I finished telling Ritchie what happened, he had this strange look on his face.

"Are you okay?" I finally asked him.

"Yep. Just shocked, I guess. You don't expect something like that to happen in a little town like this."

"Who would want to murder Walter?" I asked.

"I can think of several people who might have done it," Ritchie said, rubbing his forehead with the back of his hand.

"Really?"

Maybe things were looking up for me.

"Walter didn't have the greatest reputation when it came to loaning money to folks," Ritchie said. "A year ago, I asked him for a loan to fix up the diner."

I couldn't pass up the chance to rib him. "Were you finally getting rid of Marilyn's salt and pepper shaker collection?"

Ritchie scowled at me. Marilyn's collection was a sore point with him. When Ralph sold the diner, he told his wife she couldn't take her shakers to Florida. So, all three hundred sets of them remained behind on tiny wooden shelves that ring the outer walls of the diner. Ritchie once tried to take them down, but had to stop when customers complained. They love those shakers.

"Why did Walter turn you down?"

Ritchie's eyes flashed. "He claimed I ran a risky business. I could be sued if a customer developed food poisoning after eating my meatloaf special. I bet if you ask other business owners on the square, they'd tell you similar stories. Walter was a tightwad. He wasn't liked by most business owners."

"Funny, Mandy told me a similar story last night," I said. "He was always very generous to me."

"That's it," Ritchie said, smacking his hands on the table. "I should have worn a miniskirt and a tight sweater when I asked Walter for a loan."

I laughed out loud. Ritchie can get my endorphins going better than thirty minutes on a treadmill. And, he's a lot more fun!

"Tightwad or not," I said. "I plan to find out who murdered him. Walter was my best tipper. I'm not likely to find anyone that generous again. Besides, I don't like being called a person of interest. Everyone looks at me funny. It's creepy."

"Don't worry what other people think," Ritchie said as he stood up and headed back to the kitchen. "Don't get involved in Walter's murder. Leave that to the police."

Ritchie was right. I should let Dan, Nate, Frank and the others solve Walter's murder. But they shouldn't care if I asked people a few questions of my own. Besides, I had no intention of telling the police what I'd be up to.

I glanced at my watch. Nearly nine o'clock. Time for work. I hate being late. Before entering the diner this morning, I'd gathered the loose change in my truck's ashtray and dropped it on the lunch counter next to my partially eaten cinnamon swirl and Diet Dr. Pepper. I was now officially broke, except for a crumpled dollar in my miniskirt pocket.

Maybe I could talk Madge into a cash advance, or a new client might drop by this morning and hand me a big tip. I definitely needed another Walter Morgan in my life.

Preferably a live one!

CHAPTER 6

As I rummaged through my handbag looking for my work keys, I saw Trudy Castle already sitting at her nail station. She's the salon's other manicurist and a real brown-noser.

"Now, Candi, be nice," I imagined Madge whispering in my ear as I put my keys away. "It's a new day."

Madge was right. It was a new day. She has one rule when it comes to us girls. No cat fights in front of clients. It's a good rule. Very professional, and I usually don't have any trouble following it. But sometimes Trudy can be a real pain in my you-know-what.

Here's why. She isn't thirty yet, but she's already been a manicurist longer than I have. Trudy went to a cosmetology school in Louisville right after graduating from some high school in the hills of Kentucky. She thinks it gives her the right to tell me when I mess up. Look, I know I'm not the greatest manicurist in the world. I've only been doing it for slightly more than two years, but I always try my best. My clients don't complain too often. So, what's Trudy's problem?

"Okay, Madge," I heard myself saying out loud. "I'll be nice to Trudy, but if she says something, I may pop her." I stepped inside.

"Mornin' Trudy," I said as cheerful as I could without gagging. "You're here nice and early this morning."

"I'm always here first, Candi," Trudy replied, pushing back a lock of her wavy black hair that had fallen in front of her tiny round face. "You never noticed."

1-2-3-4…Temper, Candi. Keep it under control.

"Where's Madge?"

"She called a few minutes ago. She won big last night at one of the riverboat casinos along the Ohio River. Madge and her girlfriends stayed overnight to see if they could double their money this morning. She'll call back later."

I swear Madge Parsons is the luckiest woman in the world. She and her girlfriends visit the casinos once or twice a week. She's always coming home with a wad of cash in her purse. I wish some of her luck would rub off on me. I sometimes buy a Hoosier Lottery ticket, but it isn't exactly high stakes gambling. Specially the rub-off kind.

Trudy had already made a pot of coffee. It's for clients only, but since I didn't finish my Diet Dr. Pepper this morning, I helped myself. I usually don't drink coffee. It tastes too bitter, but I needed some caffeine to jumpstart my morning. I hardly slept at all last night.

"Have an interesting day off?" Trudy asked in her annoying nasal-sounding voice.

"Huh?"

"According to this morning's *Beacon*, you spent part of your evening at the bank."

5-6-7-8…Remember your temper, Candi.

"Don't believe everything you read in the newspaper," I snapped. "It's all a big misunderstanding. And wait until I see McPherson. I'll set him straight."

"So, what were you doing there?"

"I don't want to talk about it."

"Okay," Trudy said, glancing at our appointment book on the front counter. "You better make up a good story before Madge arrives. You know how she is. Once she reads about Walter's murder, she'll ask you a zillion questions."

Trudy was right. She's right most of the time. That's one of the things I hate about her. Madge will want to know everything that happened at the bank last night. And, I'm not looking forward to telling her the truth. It's not that I want to keep Walter's secret any longer. It's that she won't be happy when she finds out I've been opening the nail salon behind her back for the past three months.

I had half a mind to throw something at Trudy for reminding me of my pending showdown with Madge. But as I looked around for an appropriate object, Sylvia Wilson walked in.

"Good morning, ladies," she said, flashing us a wide smile.

Sylvia is a petite, silver-haired woman who taught second grade at the elementary school for years before she grew tired of disciplining her unruly pupils and their parents and retired. Now, Sylvia runs the Drayton Drake Memorial Youth Center on the east side of the town square. Drayton was a long-time Congressman and the father of our current town president, Douglas Drake.

"Where's Madge?"

"She's—"

I interrupted Trudy.

"Madge is feeling a little under the weather this morning and won't be in until later."

"Oh, my, I hope it's nothing serious," Sylvia said. She seemed genuinely concerned about Madge's sudden illness.

"No worries. It's just something that overtakes her every now and again," I said, adding, "I'm sure she'll be over it by noon."

I hated to tell Sylvia a little white lie. After all, she'd been my daughter's second grade teacher. However, I figured Madge wouldn't appreciate us girls telling folks how she spends her spare time. News like that could spread around town faster than a California wildfire. It might hurt our business. Good Christian ladies aren't supposed to gamble.

"What have you got in your hand?" I asked Sylvia, changing the subject.

"Oh, yes, it's the reason I'm here," she said. "It's a poster for our big fundraiser on Saturday night at the Foliage Festival. Would you display it in your window?"

"Sure," I said, taking the poster from her and giving it to Trudy to hang in the salon's front window.

"What type of fundraiser is it?" I asked.

"It's called a faux beauty contest."

"A what?"

"Believe me, it wasn't my idea," Sylvia said. "Douglas Drake came up with it. The rest of our board of directors reluctantly went along with him. Drayton is likely rolling over in his grave.

"Douglas has persuaded some folks to dress up in evening gowns, makeup, and big wigs and strut across the festival's main stage on Saturday night. It's weird if you ask me, but Douglas thinks people will love it and stuff money in donation baskets in front of each contestant."

"Let me get this straight," I said, shaking my head. "Dougie's putting on a drag show to raise money for the Youth Center? Darn. He was always different in high school, but this takes the cake."

"I agree," Sylvia said, craning her neck to make sure nobody else was listening to our conversation. "But I guess when you're the town president and your daddy willed the building to the Youth Center; you can do whatever you want."

"By the way, how are the renovations coming along?" I asked, sensing Sylvia was uncomfortable talking about the faux beauty pageant.

"We haven't raised as much money as we wanted since the electrical fire in June, but if we do well enough on Saturday night, we can finish the final repairs and re-open before the holidays."

I reached into the pocket of my miniskirt and pulled out my crumpled dollar bill and handed it to Sylvia. I was now officially broke.

"It's not much," I said, "but when I get paid later this week, I'll donate more at the faux beauty contest. That will be something to see." I chuckled a bit as I imagined my ex in a leopard print gown wearing red stilettos and my rabbit fur jacket. I definitely would check out this event.

"Thanks, Candi," Sylvia said, taking my dollar. "Every little bit helps. I should get going. I have more posters to pass out. By the way, I hope everything works out with you and what took place at the bank last night."

"You've read the paper, too," I replied. "Seems everyone in town did this morning. I didn't have anything to do with Walter's murder."

"I believe you, Candi. I was shocked, too. Anybody who raised such a polite little girl like Jenny couldn't be mixed up in Walter's death"

"Thanks for mentioning her," I said, smiling. "She's all grown up. Married, with two kids of her own, Jacob and Abby. I'm a grandmother, can you believe that?"

"Goodness me, how time flies," Sylvia said as she left the salon. "You're too young to be a grandmother."

Ain't that the truth?

CHAPTER 7

fter finishing with my 10:30 client, I told Trudy I was taking an early lunch. I needed to check the bank's ATM machine to see if I had any money left in my savings account.

"Whatever," Trudy replied, looking up from the magazine she was reading.

The sun shone brightly as I stepped into the street. I decided to walk across the square to the bank. Several town workers were raking leaves at the side of the courthouse lawn, but stopped as I passed by. They were also cleaning the courthouse parking lot so vendors could erect their tents on Wednesday night for the start of the town's annual Foliage Festival.

As I made a beeline for the ATM machine, I spotted someone entering the bank. That's odd, I thought. Shouldn't the bank be closed out of respect for Walter's passing? I decided to step inside to see what was going on.

Louise Dorfman was busy counting the money in her till. She has worked part-time at the bank forever. As a teenager, I'd stopped by each week to hand her the quarters I earned from babysitting my younger half-brother, Randy, and the other kids at the Shady Pines Mobile Home Park where we lived for several years. I was saving for a shiny two-wheeler, but never bought one. It was one of those times when Mom lost her job for being late all the time, and we needed my savings to help pay our rent.

"Hi, Candi," Louise said. "Here to give us some money?"

"I wish. No, I came to see if I had any left in my savings account. Otherwise, I'll need to declare bankruptcy." I laughed as if I were joking. I wish.

Louise smiled and shifted slightly on her stool as she looked up my account on her computer.

"Looks like you're still solvent," she said, writing my balance on a slip of paper and sliding it across the counter to me.

"What do you know, I'm rich. In that case, give me a twenty."

I filled out a withdrawal slip while Louise opened her money drawer and handed me a crisp twenty-dollar bill.

"I read in this morning's paper that you found Walter's body in his office last night," Louise said. "Is that right?"

"Yup, lucky me" I replied, shoving the twenty in my jacket pocket.

"We've known each other forever, right?" Louise said, clearing her throat. "Mind if I ask you a personal question?"

"Sure, fire away."

I had no idea what Louise was about to ask me. My personal life is pretty boring. All I do is work, watch TV at night, and sleep, which isn't always possible. Every two or three weeks I drive to Indianapolis on the weekend to visit my daughter, Jenny Gibson, and my grandbabies. With a life like this, I won't be getting my own reality TV show anytime soon.

"I don't know a delicate way to ask this question," Louise said, lowering her voice so the teller and customer standing next to us couldn't hear. "The police told Jane Parker that Walter was stabbed in the back with a hunting knife. Is that true?"

"Afraid so."

"Goodness gracious, you must have been frightened out of your mind."

"Let me put it this way, Louise. It's a sight I never want to see again. Can I ask you a question? Why is the bank open? I would have thought…."

"It was Jane Parker's idea. She talked to Chief Cobb and Irene Morgan late last night. Since everything happened in Walter's office, out of public view, there was no reason to close the bank. Jane called everyone early this morning and asked us to come to work as usual. She was worried people would panic after learning of Walter's murder. Maybe withdraw all their money. So far, that hasn't happened, thank goodness."

"That makes sense. Thanks, Louise. I'd better get back to work."

As I prepared to leave, I heard someone call my name. I looked to my left and found myself staring at Jane Parker.

"Do you have a minute to chat?" she asked, grabbing my hand. She had a firm handshake.

I nodded and followed Jane into her office. Once there, she shut her door and invited me to sit in one of the chairs next to her desk. They weren't as nice as the ones in Walter's office, but they hadn't come from Goodwill either.

"What would you like to talk about?" I asked Jane. No sense wasting time chit chatting about the weather or this weekend's Foliage Festival. I needed to get back to the nail salon before Madge came home from the riverboat. Trudy was right. I'd have some explaining to do about last night.

At first, Jane, the bank's second in command, sat in her comfy leather chair and smiled at me. She has perfect shiny white teeth. Like she just had a dental check-up. Jane also has a perfect hairdo with expensive-looking blonde streaks running through her jet-black hair. Not a lock out of place. Let's be honest here. I hate women like her who look perfect all the time.

"I heard you found poor Walter last night," Jane said, straightening the sides of her chic red blazer. "Chief Cobb filled me in on what happened, but I'm still curious about a few things."

"Like, what?"

"Well, for instance, I don't know how to say this delicately. What were you doing in Walter's office?"

"Dan didn't tell you?"

"No, but then again, I couldn't find a dignified way to bring it up in my conversation with him. But I'm still curious nevertheless, you understand."

"Well, it's like this Miz Parker," I began. "I've been treating Walter's hangnail problem on a weekly basis for the past three months. When he didn't show up at the nail salon last night, I came looking for him."

"I see," Jane said, her eyes growing wide. She began fiddling with her gold-colored letter opener.

"You seem surprised that Walter was having his nails done, Miz Parker."

"It's just that Walter was so old fashioned in so many ways," Jane said, putting one of her own well-manicured fingers to her lips to repress a smile. "I can't imagine him going to a nail salon."

"You'd be surprised how many men have their nails done these days," I said, defending my profession. "Not here in Bartonsville, of course, but in bigger places like Indianapolis or Chicago. Some men don't consider it a sissy thing anymore. Besides, Walter had terrible hangnails."

"I guess that solves the mystery," Jane said. "Did Walter mention why he skipped his appointment last night?"

"No, he keeled over on his desk when I walked in. Why was he working so late last night?"

"I can't tell you. Banks are subject to strict privacy laws. Incidentally, Chief Cobb mentioned Walter was wearing pink nail polish. Is that true?"

"Yup, but I didn't paint his nails if that's what you're thinking."

"Sorry, I wasn't implying anything," Jane said, who seemed embarrassed at asking her question. "It's just that you're a manicurist and everything. You understand. I was curious."

"That's okay," I said as I stood up and headed for Jane's door. "By the way, I couldn't help but notice your own lovely red nails. Next time, you think about having them done, drop by Tips & Toes, and we'll give you a good deal."

Before heading back to work, I picked up a grilled cheese sandwich and a medium Diet Dr. Pepper at Ralph's. As I waited for my order, I glanced to my right and noticed J. William McPherson sitting in the rear booth.

"Well, if it isn't Candi DeCarlo," McPherson said, looking up at me from his cheeseburger deluxe platter.

"We need to talk, McPherson."

"Fine. Sit down. I need to ask you a few questions myself."

I was seated only a minute when Joanie dropped off my lunch.

"Let me know if you need anything else, Hon," she said, winking at me.

I nodded. It was Joanie's way of telling me that if I decided to go across the table at McPherson's throat, she'd have my back. Waitress solidarity forever. I took a bite of my grilled cheese and told McPherson he could ask the first question.

"Okay, let's try this one. What were you doing inside Walter's bank last night?"

"I'm not answering that question on the grounds it may tend to incriminate me."

I heard a guy use that line one night on C-Span as I was flipping through my cable TV channels. Beads of sweat had formed on his forehead and he looked guilty as hell.

"Taking the fifth, huh?" McPherson said, wiping a blob of mustard off his chin. "Well, how about this question. Is it true Walter Morgan killed himself?"

"It's not my job to tell you what happened."

"So, he didn't kill himself," McPherson said, pounding the table with his beefy fist. "I knew it."

"Why do you say that?"

"I have sources," McPherson said.

"Sources, huh? Johnny Edwards, right?"

"How'd you know that?"

"'Cause he was sitting in his wheelchair when Nate Sloan and I walked out of the bank last night."

"He's a trusted source," McPherson said. "Johnny used to be a journalist himself. He worked part-time at WYMN."

Two can play this game. I threw my facts right back in his face. "Yeah, that was before Martha Rae Folger, the station's general manager, fired him for getting too many facts wrong in the stories he covered."

"So, if Walter didn't commit suicide, and you didn't kill him, who did?"

"Who knows?" I said. "Now, I have a question for you, McPherson."

"Fire away."

"Did the new police chief tell you I was a person of inter-est, or did you make that up on your own?"

"I'm deeply offended, Candi, I'm a professional journalist. I usually don't make up quotes. That's what Chief Cobb told me or was it Johnny? I don't remember exactly. I was on a deadline and sometimes I don't always write people's answers down in my notebook. However, I remember the Chief asking me a couple of questions about you."

"Like what?"

"He wanted to know if you were married or seeing anyone."

"And what did you tell him?"

"I wasn't your appointment secretary. He'd have to ask you himself."

Hmmm. I knew it. I made an impression on Dan. Candi, you haven't lost it yet, girl. Wait till I tell Mandy.

"Sorry, but I gotta end this delightful conversation," McPherson said, stuffing the last bite of his cheeseburger in his mouth. "I have more interviews to conduct. But, before I forget, I couldn't use your age in my story this morning. How old are you anyway?"

"Wouldn't you love to know, McPherson."

CHAPTER 8

It was nearly one-thirty before I made it back to Tips & Toes. Trudy wasn't back from her own lunch break or wherever she had gone, but fortunately, no clients were waiting for us.

"Well…well. The prodigal manicurist has finally returned," Madge said from atop her wooden stool.

"Did Trudy tell you Walter Morgan was murdered last night, and I was in his bank shortly after it happened?"

"What? Walter was murdered?"

Madge was so excited she nearly fell off her perch. Madge hates being the last person in town to know anything. Especially if it's juicy like the murder of one of the town's bigwigs.

Hmmm?

If Madge didn't know about Walter, then Trudy hadn't said anything to her while I was gone. I didn't know whether to hug Trudy or throw something at her when she got back.

"What's going on?" Madge said as she placed both elbows on the front counter and waited for me to spill the rest.

I moved closer and took my sweet time mentioning everything that happened after finding Walter dead in his office last night. When I finished, Madge had a funny look on her face. Like I had been speaking in tongues.

"What's wrong?" I asked.

"Why were you inside the bank last night?"

Uh-oh. I had hoped Madge wouldn't pick up on that point. Especially after I spent most of my time describing the gruesome details of Walter's murder. Guess I'm not that lucky. I needed to come up with a story fast. Should I tell Madge what I told the cops last night, or the truth?

What's that old expression about the third time being a charm? When I finished my fib, Madge looked at me and said, "But nobody's ever asked us about a gift certificate before."

"Exactly, and it's why I thought Walter was onto something."

"You're right," she said, a big smile forming across her pudgy face. "Maybe I should get busy and make up some gift certificates. They'll make great Christmas stocking stuffers."

Madge had bought my story. But I couldn't let our conversation end.

"Have any idea why someone would murder Walter?" I asked.

"Probably for the same reason everyone else in town wanted to kill him," Madge said. "He wouldn't loan them any money."

"That's interesting. Everybody I've talked to so far has given me the same answer," I said. "Was he a tightwad like everyone says?"

"That's what I've heard," Madge offered. "Fortunately, I've never asked him for a loan. My dear Harold left me plenty of money before he died."

Trudy came back from lunch a few minutes later. Madge announced it was her turn to grab something to eat. She wasn't gone more than a few minutes when Trudy saddled up to me.

"Did Madge buy your story?"

"About being at the bank last night? Sure, why wouldn't she?"

Trudy shrugged. "Did she tell you her news?"

"What's that?" I asked.

Trudy loves it when she knows something I don't know.

"Madge is giving the salon a makeover."

"What?"

"She's taking her winnings from the riverboat last night and remodeling the salon. One of her best friends, Helen Sloan, is setting up a table or two in here to sell her cosmetics. From now on, Madge says the place will be known as Madge and Helen's Beauty Emporium."

"Wait a minute," I said. "That's nuts. They can't. That'll ruin everything. Just wait till Madge gets back."

I didn't have to wait long. Madge was back with a takeout carton from the diner. When I spotted her, I stomped up to the front counter where she was now seated, enjoying her tuna fish sandwich. It smelled.

"What's this about giving the salon a makeover?" I asked.

"Oops, I forgot to mention it when we were talking about poor Walter," Madge said, biting into her sandwich. "It's true, honey. I've decided to spruce up the place. Here, I'll show you what it will look like."

Madge jumped down off her stool and pulled a magazine from underneath the front counter.

"Look here," she said, spreading the magazine on the counter-top. "What do you think of these colors?"

I glanced at the magazine photo spread. It showed a Beverly Hills beauty shop with wide purple strips running sideways down bright yellow walls.

"Aren't those colors too bright for us?" I said. "Our clients are old. They're used to our dull beige walls."

"I know, honey, but times are changing. Our clients won't be with us forever," Madge said, tilting her eyes heavenward. "We have to accept that fact of life. We need to embrace new demographics. Seize the moment. I read all about it in *Salon Owner's Monthly* a few weeks ago."

Whew. I was relieved. For a minute, I thought Ritchie had served Madge a bad tuna fish sandwich. Or, her hormones were out of whack because she forgot to take her meds on her gambling trip.

"You shouldn't change our name. Everybody knows us as Tips & Toes. Madge and Helen's Beauty Emporium? It sounds too much like a beauty shop."

"Trudy's been blabbing to you, hasn't she? I told her that in confidence. Oh, well, you'd have found out soon enough. Yes, I'm changing our name. I want to help promote Helen's business. The best way is to call ourselves Madge and Helen's Beauty Emporium. We can use Walter's idea of selling gift certificates. We'll have so much more to offer our clients once Helen moves in."

I wanted to continue arguing with Madge, but I know a lost cause when I see one. She obviously had made up her mind. And Madge wasn't likely to change it for anything. She's a stubborn old woman.

"Did Madge fill you in on her plans?" Trudy asked, after I walked back to my nail station.

"Yup, and I told her about my own plans."

"Are you quitting?"

Trudy had a stupid smirk on her face. Like her prayers finally had been answered, and I wouldn't be any more competition for her.

"Sorry, it's nothing like that," I said. "Madge is thinking too small. She needs to be more creative. The sky's the limit."

"What are you talking about?" Trudy said, shaking her head.

"Chili sauce."

"Huh?"

"I've persuaded Madge to let me start selling my late Grandma Thompson's famous chili sauce," I said. "I'm rushing home right after work to make a batch."

"You're doing what?"

I smiled. I had Trudy's full attention.

"Chili sauce," I repeated. "Grandma made the best chili sauce in Barton County. She was always winning blue ribbons at the annual county fair."

Trudy stormed past me and nearly knocked over Lonnie Sparks, my eighty-year-old client, who was about to sit down at my nail station.

"What's all the fuss about?" Lonnie asked.

I quickly filled her in on Madge's plans to remodel the salon as I dipped Lonnie's fingernails in a soapy solution to soften them. When I finished, she looked straight at me.

"I swear Madge could screw up a one-horse parade if someone would let her."

I smiled. Lonnie had a point. We'll have to wait and see what happens. I asked Lonnie if she'd heard about Walter Morgan's murder.

"Yeah, it was all over the radio on WYMN on my way here," she said. "I know one thing. The cops will be busy interviewing everyone who ever thought of murdering Walter. I hear it's a long list."

"That's what I've heard, too," I said as I gave Lonnie a new set of French nails.

A half hour after she left, Madge wandered back to my station.

"Why'd you lie to Trudy about your grandma's chili sauce? You've got her all upset. Now, she wants to sell her crochet work in the salon. Why do you persist in upsetting her all the time?"

It's fun?

I shrugged and grinned at Madge.

"Don't do it again, okay? Trudy and I are leaving early. We're stopping by Lowe's to pick out the paint for the makeover. I've talked to my nephew. He's stopping by tomorrow morning to start scraping and painting. Can you close up the salon tonight and drop off the night deposit at the bank?"

"Sure." *And can I pick up your dry cleaning, too?*

CHAPTER 9

As I finished preparing the night deposit, I heard the tiny bell over the salon's front door ring. Anne Taylor, a tall, skinny news reporter for one of the Indianapolis TV stations, stormed in. She was wearing an expensive-looking beige London Fog trench coat tied securely around her virtually non-existent waist. Following her into the salon was a burly guy juggling a heavy-looking camera on his right shoulder and a smaller dude with some sound equipment in his hands.

"Hi," Anne said, flashing me a toothy smile. I hoped it wouldn't crack her heavily made-up face. "I'm Anne Taylor from Action News. Are you Candi DeCarlo? I want to talk to you about finding Walter Morgan murdered in his office last night."

"Sorry, you just missed Candi," I replied with a straight face." She left with our owner, Madge Parsons. They had to buy some supplies for the salon. They won't be back until tomorrow."

"Darn," Anne said. "What's your name? What do you do here?"

"My name is Trudy Castle," I replied. "I'm a manicurist here."

"Anne," her cameraman said. "Hurry and decide if you want to interview this person. Our live remote is less than five minutes away."

"All right, Jerry, give me a minute," Anne said. "I need to decide if it's worth talking to her. Our news director will be mad if we don't interview someone. Too bad Chief Cobb didn't have any time for us."

"I'm sorry to hear about that," I said. "Dan is very photogenic."

"Tell me about it," Anne replied. "I once dated him when he was a homicide detective with the Indianapolis Metropolitan Police Department."

She dated Dan? Did he take her to dinner and a movie? Did he give her a goodnight kiss? Was he a good kisser? Inquiring minds wanted to know.

Anne, however, wasn't paying any attention. She was too busy staring at herself in the large mirror behind our front counter. She pulled a hairbrush out of her tiny Coach purse and ran it through her shoulder-length blonde hair several times before reapplying her red lipstick.

"Okay, I'm ready," she said. "Let's do the interview outside. Can you follow us there? What was your name again?"

"Trudy," I said. "Trudy Castle."

Once in front of the nail salon, Anne waited for a cue in her earpiece before she shoved a microphone in my face and asked, "Can you tell us how Candi DeCarlo felt after finding Walter Morgan in his office last night?"

"Candi was devastated," I replied. "Walter Morgan was such a wonderful man."

"What was Miz DeCarlo doing inside the bank?" Anne asked. "Chief Cobb's office told us the crime occurred there after hours."

Here we go again.

"You need to understand that Candi is one of the most dedicated manicurists in our profession," I said. "She went to the bank Monday night, on her day off no less. Mister Morgan wanted to buy a salon gift certificate for his wife's upcoming birthday."

"Thank you, Miz Castle," Anne said as she looked directly into the camera. "The tragic murder of Walter Morgan has gripped the residents of Bartonsville. As they mourn the loss of one of its leading citizens, residents are fearful a cold-blooded killer may still be on the loose, roaming the streets of this quaint little town looking for his next victim. For Action News, this is Anne Taylor reporting. Back to you in the studio."

Anne again thanked me for the interview before jumping into the TV van and driving away with her crew. I stepped back into the nail salon, grabbed the night deposit off the counter before exiting and locking the front door.

"Hi, Candi."

Johnny Edwards was sitting there in his motorized wheelchair.

"What are you doing here?"

"I owe you an apology," he said before handing me a single red rose.

"Finally decided to fess up? You were the anonymous source in McPherson's story, weren't you?"

"Yes, I called him last night after spotting you and Nate leaving the bank. I told him something was up, and he needed to get on the story right away. I didn't think he'd print your name in the paper."

"Well, I hope you've learned a valuable lesson from this experience."

"What's that?"

"Never trust a reporter."

"But, I once worked as one for Martha Rae Folger at the radio station."

"I know. By the way, did you see my interview with Anne Taylor?"

"Was that who that person was?" Johnny asked. "I could see you talking to a TV reporter, but I was still a block away."

"Yeah, it was my first TV interview."

"How did it go?"

"I lied and told her my name was Trudy Castle. And, how Candi had already left the nail salon."

"Why did you do that?" Johnny asked.

"I dunno. She showed up unexpectedly. I panicked, okay? Besides, who wants TV reporters knocking on your front door? Not me. Now, if you'll excuse me, I need to drop off our night deposit before I drive home. Thanks for the rose. It's lovely. I also accept your apology."

"Okay, but can I ask you one more question?"

"On or off the record?"

"Off the record," he said. "Who murdered Walter? After talking to several people in town today, it sounds like it could have been anyone."

"I came to the same conclusion. Walter apparently was a tightwad when it came to lending money to the businessowners in town."

"Well, I intend to find out who did it," Johnny said, sitting taller in his wheelchair.

"What are you now? A private detective?"

"Maybe."

CHAPTER 10

After thanking Johnny again for the rose, I hopped into my truck and spun halfway around the square to the State Bank of Bartonsville, where I dropped the night deposit in an outside slot next to the main entrance. A minute later, I heard my cell phone inside my handbag, grabbed it and answered.

"Where have you been?" Mandy asked. "I let it ring at least a half dozen times."

What's got her so excited?

"I had to drop off our night deposit after doing an interview with Anne Taylor."

"That overly made-up TV news bimbo from Indianapolis?"

"Yeah, she wondered what it felt like to find Walter murdered inside his office."

"What did you tell her?"

"I used my old gift certificate line on her. I also told her my name was Trudy Castle."

"Why did you do that?"

"I don't know. Seemed like it might be fun to mess with her. By the way, did you know Anne once dated Dan Cobb."

"Our new police chief?"

"Yeah, I wanted to ask about her date, but she was on deadline. So, why were you so anxious to chat with me?"

"Haven't you heard the latest?"

"What? No, wait a minute, let me guess. You just won the Hoosier Lottery?"

"I don't play the lottery. I'm already rich. No, the police have arrested Sylvia Wilson for Walter Morgan's murder."

"What? Who told you that?"

"Nate Sloan," Mandy said. "He pulled me over a half hour ago for speeding on the south side of town. I was sitting in his cruiser waiting for him to finish writing me a speeding ticket when the word came over his police radio."

"That's impossible," I said, leaning back in my seat. "Sylvia couldn't have done it. She can't be more than five feet tall. Walter was more than six feet. She'd have had to use a step ladder to stick the hunting knife in his back."

"Good point, Candi. Maybe she had help."

"That's possible, but I doubt it. Let me see what I can find out, and I'll call you right back."

After Mandy hung up, I asked myself how I could learn more about Sylvia's arrest. Then it hit me. Of course, Mary

Donovan. I'll call the police station and ask her. She'll tell me. My clients don't keep secrets from me.

"Good evening, Bartonsville Police Department, how can we assist you?" Mary said in a professional sounding voice.

"Mary, it's me, Candi."

"Ah, the lovely, Miz DeCarlo," Mary said. "How can we help you this evening? Wait, don't tell me. You've found another body for us, have you?"

Mary is such a kidder.

"Sorry to disappoint you, Mary. I'm calling to confirm your appointment for tomorrow afternoon. I've got you down for three."

"I thought it was three-thirty. But, I'll be there, regardless. So, tell me, Candi, why are you calling to remind me of my appointment? You've never done that before."

There she goes again. Too smart for her own good. Mary was right. I've never called clients before.

"It's something Madge wants us to start doing. She's worried our clients are getting older and more forgetful. She wants to make sure they show up when they're supposed to."

"Are you putting me in that category, Candi?"

"No, no, Mary. Of course not. It's Madge. You know how she is sometimes."

I decided to move on.

"So, is there anything going on around town tonight?"

"As a matter of fact, several folks are patiently waiting on my other lines. I don't mean to be rude, but I need to take their calls. Maybe one of them has found us a body. Thanks for calling. I'll see you tomorrow at three-thirty."

Darn, I didn't get the chance to ask Mary about Sylvia Wilson. I sat in my truck and thought. If the police arrested Sylvia for Walter's murder, they probably took her to the county jail. On Monday night, Dan said the town's holding cells were being renovated this week. If I drove out to the county jail, I could meet Sylvia and learn what's going on with her.

The county jail is on the western edge of town. A five-minute drive. The parking gods were on my side tonight. I parked in front of the two-story red brick building and walked inside.

"What can I do for you?" asked the chunky, middle-aged officer leaning against the jail's front counter. He'd been glancing through a magazine and suddenly looked flustered as I approached. He'd probably been reading a girlie magazine.

"I need to see Sylvia Wilson," I said politely.

Fatso gave me a quick once over with his beady little eyes while trying to stash his magazine underneath some folders on the counter.

"Are you a family member?" he asked suspiciously.

"Why does that matter?"

"Cause nobody but a family member or her attorney can speak to her."

"But I'm a friend of hers. She taught my daughter in second grade."

"That's nice, lady. I'm happy that you and your daughter might know a cold-blooded murderer. But I have my orders. Straight from Sheriff J.D. Pickle himself. Nobody but family members or her attorney can see Sylvia Wilson."

I considered telling fatso I was Sylvia's court-appointed attorney, but he'd probably never seen a lawyer in a miniskirt and a fur jacket before. For that matter, neither had I.

I began walking away. But I stopped halfway to the front door, looked over my left shoulder, and said, "By the way, what's your name?"

"You talking to me?" the officer said, while retrieving his girlie magazine. "It's McIntyre. Want I should spell it for you?"

"No, thanks. I've got it."

Once outside, I pulled out my cell phone and dialed 9-1-1.

"Good evening, Bartonsville Police Department. What is your emergency?"

"Mary?"

"Is that you again, Candi?" Mary asked. "Well, I've got news for you. I haven't forgotten my nail appointment. It's at three-thirty, right?"

"I'm not calling about that. I need a favor."

"Where are you?"

I told Mary my whereabouts and who I wanted to see.

"Who said you couldn't talk to Sylvia?"

"Some fat guy named McIntyre."

"Dexter McIntyre. He's such a big blowhard. Give me a minute to set him straight."

I did what Mary told me. I sat down on a wooden bench next to the jail's front entrance and waited five minutes. Then, I stood up and walked back inside.

This should be fun.

CHAPTER 11

Dexter McIntyre glared at me as I approached the front counter again.

"Grab a seat over there, lady," he snapped and pointed to a row of plastic chairs along the far wall. "It'll take a few minutes to bring your friend up front."

I sat down and waited patiently. I wondered what Mary said to McIntyre to have him ignore a direct order. And from Sheriff J.D. Pickle, no less. One more thing to ask her when she showed up for her nail appointment tomorrow.

Five minutes passed before McIntyre told me to walk down the hallway to his left and stop at the second interrogation room on the right.

"Hi, Sylvia," I said as I walked through the doorway a minute later. The room wasn't much bigger than my bathroom. The walls were painted an icky lime green color. Martha Stewart would not approve.

Sylvia was hunched over a small wooden table in the middle of the room, her long gray hair, which she usually wears up, practically touched the table. She was wearing an orange jumpsuit with the words "Barton County Jail" stenciled in black lettering across the back. It made her look even smaller than normal. A guard, who could have passed for Dexter's twin, stood in the corner behind the door, his arms resting on his large midsection.

"Candi," Sylvia said, looking up from the table. She seemed surprised to see me.

"What's going on?" I replied, sitting down on a chair across from her.

"I don't know," Sylvia said in a low voice. "Two officers dropped by the Youth Center yesterday afternoon. They said Chief Cobb wanted to see me about Walter's murder. They then drove me to the police station for questioning. After about an hour, the Chief said he was holding me on suspicion of murder. Then, they brought me here. I'm apparently being formally charged in front of Judge Randall Stone tomorrow morning."

"What?" I said, shaking my head. "Dan can't believe you murdered Walter, can he?"

"On the way here, one of the officers said Chief Cobb found some incriminating evidence on Walter's desk."

"What kind of evidence?"

"The officer didn't say."

"Got any idea what it could be?"

"No, but there's something else I haven't told you yet."

"What's that?"

"After the police picked me up, they went through my purse at the station and found a tiny bottle of nail polish inside."

I glanced at Sylvia's nails. They were bare.

"Let me guess," I said, leaning back in my chair. "Was it a bottle of Essie #422?"

"That could be the name they mentioned," Sylvia said. "I don't use nail polish. It causes me to break out in a rash."

I banged both hands on the table.

"What's wrong, Candi?"

"Don't you see. Somebody's framing you for Walter's murder."

"Why would they do that?" Sylvia asked with a perplexed look on her face.

"I don't know, but I plan to find out. There's also something I need to ask. Do you own a hunting knife?"

"Heavens, no. Why would you ask me such a ridiculous question?"

"Because when I found Walter inside his office last night, a large hunting knife was sticking out of the middle of his back. And, his fingernails were painted with pink nail polish."

"Oh, my goodness, that's horrible."

"We need to find out who slipped that bottle of nail polish into your purse. Where were you yesterday?"

"Everywhere," Sylvia said. "I spent most of the day asking businesses on the town square to put one of our posters in their front windows. Maybe somebody dropped the nail polish in my purse along the way. Think that's possible?"

"It could be. Write down all the stores you visited, and I'll check them out."

"Okay," she said, grabbing the pen and piece of paper I removed from my handbag.

"That's enough for now, lady," the guard said when Sylvia finished writing out her list. He moved away from the wall he'd been holding up for the past fifteen minutes and was now hovering over me. By the look on his face, I could tell that if I didn't leave right away, he'd toss me out on my ears. I got the message. I stood up, grabbed the paper and pen out of Sylvia's hand and gently patted her arm.

"Don't worry, Sylvia, I'll get to the bottom of this."

As I drove home, I wondered how to keep my promise to Sylvia without Dan finding out. I parked my truck in front of my second-floor apartment on Elm Street. After checking my mailbox for bills, I climbed the twenty-plus steps to my front door.

The red light on my answering machine in the kitchen was blinking as I stepped inside. Who could that be? I hit the play button. Jane Parker from the State Bank of Bartonsville asked me to drop by tomorrow if I had time. She wanted to talk, but she didn't say why.

Hmmm?

Maybe Jane wants to make a nail appointment. It was either that or my checking account was overdrawn again. I hadn't written a check since last Saturday. But I was too tired to worry about it now.

I poured myself a Diet Dr. Pepper, flipped on my TV, and settled into my rocking chair in the living room. My plan was to watch the boob tube for a half hour before crawling into bed. However, the next sound I heard was my answering machine clicking off.

I shuffled into the kitchen and punched the machine's play button. It was Mandy. I hit the speed dial. She answered on the second ring.

"Where have you been?" she asked. "I called earlier, but you didn't answer."

I told Mandy about visiting the county jail and interviewing Sylvia Wilson.

"Does Sylvia have an attorney yet?" Mandy asked when I finished.

"I don't know. We got caught up in the details of her arrest, and I forgot to ask her."

"She probably doesn't have much money, so when she appears in court tomorrow, the judge will assign her a public defender. That's like asking a blind Boy Scout to help her across the street.

"Public defenders don't know anything. I'd rather see her with a real attorney. Let me call my friend, Carol Hansen."

"Carol's terrific. She handled my divorce from Bobby."

"That's right. She'll make sure Sylvia doesn't get the runaround from the prosecutor or the cops until we can find her a real criminal defense attorney."

"That's so sweet of you," I said, "Why are you doing it?"

"I dunno," Mandy said. "I remember how Sylvia comforted Jenny when you and Bobby first began having problems with your marriage. How Jenny confided in Sylvia about the awful things Bobby said about you, especially after you separated."

"Sylvia was very understanding of the whole situation. She didn't want Jenny to become traumatized by what was happening. I must have repressed it."

"That's water under the bridge now. Jenny's fine and has a wonderful family of her own. Let's see what we can do to help Sylvia. By the way, I saw you on the six o'clock news."

"How did I look? Overweight? How sincere did I sound in talking about myself?"

"You sounded like the most thoughtful manicurist in the world, but Trudy may react differently if she watched the news."

After Mandy hung up, I turned off the TV, plodded into the bedroom, threw on a nightshirt, and crawled into bed. I grabbed Freddy, my brown teddy bear, and held him close.

"Mommy's found herself in the middle of a real mess, Freddy. I sure hope it all works out."

I must have fallen asleep right away because I don't recall hearing Freddy's answer.

CHAPTER 12

"I'll have two scrambled eggs and three strips of crispy bacon today," I told Joanie before sitting at the diner's lunch counter on Wednesday morning

"Is that what TV celebrities eat for breakfast?" she replied. "I saw you on the news last night. By the way, when did you change your name?"

"I didn't. I was nervous and Trudy's name suddenly popped into my head. How did I look and sound? I've heard TV cameras make you look ten pounds heavier."

"You looked fine," Joanie said. "The camera guy shot you from the chest up."

"Great. My best parts."

"So, why are you in such a good mood this morning?"

"You're looking at someone who is embarking on an important mission."

"A mission, huh? Wait a minute. Is there a new man in your life?"

"No, nothing like that. Of course, I'd be okay if that happened, but no new man today. My mission is like one of those humanitarian stories you sometimes see on TV."

"Oh, my gosh, Candi, don't tell me you've suddenly found religion and are moving to Africa, or some other place like that to help the needy?"

"No, I interviewed Sylvia Wilson at the county jail last night. I'm convinced she didn't murder Walter Morgan, so I'm starting a legal defense fund for her."

"A legal defense fund, huh," Joanie said, placing my eggs, bacon, and a Diet Dr. Pepper in front of me. "How do you plan to start this fund?"

"Haven't figured that out yet," I said, taking a swig of my drink. "Mandy's asking Carol Hansen to represent Sylvia in court this morning, but she'll need to hire a real criminal defense attorney. Some hotshot from Indianapolis. And he won't be cheap."

"I've got an idea," Joanie said, leaning across the counter. "Make up some donation jars and have the business owners on the square stick them next to their cash registers."

"That's a terrific idea, Joanie. Why didn't I think of that? But, where can I find donation jars?"

"It's your lucky day. Ritchie finally cleaned out our storage room early this morning. He threw some empty plastic pickle jars in a garbage bag and tossed them in the dumpster out back. You can dig the jars out of the dumpster."

I quickly finished my breakfast and Diet Dr. Pepper before walking through the kitchen and into the alley. Ritchie was busy making another batch of his famous cinnamon swirls and didn't even notice me.

The lid on the diner's blue dumpster was open. Good. I wouldn't have to open it by myself. I took Mandy's advice from Monday night and wore black slacks and a purple cotton sweater underneath my rabbit fur jacket today. I took off the jacket and carefully hung it on the edge of the dumpster. No sense getting stains on it while wading through the garbage bags. I grabbed two blue plastic milk crates next to the diner's back door and used them as a step ladder to boost myself over the front lip of the dumpster.

I had sorted through most of the trash bags when I heard a male voice shout, "Ma'am, please step out of there."

I peeked over the edge of the dumpster. Dan was staring at me.

"Oh hi, Dan. What are you doing here?" I asked, lifting my left leg over the edge of the dumpster and lowering myself onto the milk crates.

"Shouldn't I be asking you that?" Dan replied, grabbing my arm so I wouldn't fall. "I listened to a call on my scanner while driving to work. Someone reported seeing what appeared to be an unidentified animal climbing into the dumpster behind Ralph's Diner. But I see now the caller was mistaken. He spotted your jacket. So, what are you doing in the dumpster?"

I didn't want to tell Dan my real reason for dumpster diving, so I made up a little story.

"It's like this. I was sitting at the lunch counter, enjoying breakfast, when I suddenly noticed that my wallet was missing. I mentioned it to Joanie, and she replied, 'oh, my goodness, Candi, I must have picked up your wallet by accident and threw it into a green trash bag when I was cleaning the dirty napkins and newspapers off the front counter.' So, that's why I'm here."

"I see," Dan replied in a voice that sounded like he hadn't completely bought my story. "Have you found your wallet yet?"

"No. But I still need to check a few more trash bags. I'm sure it will turn up in one of them."

"Good luck with your search. Before I go, I have another question. I understand you met Sylvia Wilson at the county jail last night. Is that correct?"

"How'd you know that?"

"Sheriff Pickle called me at home. He told me Mary Donovan ordered his deputy to let some woman interview Sylvia Wilson. The woman was dressed in a miniskirt and a cheap-looking fur coat. I figured it had to be you."

Cheap-looking fur coat? Wait until I see that blowhard Dexter McIntyre again!

"It wasn't Mary's fault. I made her do it. Don't be mad at her."

"I'll deal with Mary later, but why did you want to talk with Miss Wilson?"

"Sylvia didn't murderWalter Morgan. I wanted to offer her some moral support. After all, she taught my daughter in second grade. She's also done a wonderful job of managing the Youth Center."

"I see," Dan said, looking sternly at me with his gorgeous, heart-melting eyes. "You're not trying to solve Mister Morgan's murder, are you?"

"No. That's your job."

"That's right. It is my job. We have the right person for his murder."

"Whatever. But, I have a question for you."

I really wanted to ask him about his date with Anne Taylor of Action News. But then I'd have to explain how I knew and it could become complicated.

"What's your question?"

"Remember, when you told me on Monday night how you didn't think I could have killed Walter on my own?"

"I don't recall saying that."

"Well, you did. I've been thinking about it ever since. Walter was over six feet tall. I'm five eight in my stilettoes, and Sylvia's not quite five-feet. How could she overtake Walter and stab him in his back with a hunting knife? She would have needed a step ladder."

"That's an interesting theory," Dan said, rubbing his chin. "However, we discovered some incriminating evidence on Walter's desk. It strongly points in Sylvia's direction. We also found a bottle of nail polish in her purse."

Dan had it all wrong. Sylvia didn't use nail polish. Instead of saying anything more, I would find out on my own how the bottle ended up in her purse.

"I hope you find your wallet, Candi," Dan said as he walked away.

"Oh, Dan, do you mind?" I asked, extending my arm so he could steady me as I climbed back into the dumpster.

I love his warm hands—even if they do send chills down my back.

CHAPTER 13

"What's going on?" I asked, tiptoeing around a maze of boxes stacked inside the salon's doorway.

"'Mornin' Candi," Madge replied from behind the front counter. "Helen's moving in today. She wants to be ready for business before the Foliage Festival begins tomorrow."

"But I thought your nephew was painting everything first."

"He will once he and his friend show up. What's in your hands?"

"Some plastic jars I picked up at the diner."

"I hope you're not filling them with your grandma's chili sauce, are you? Remember, you can't sell chili sauce in the salon. I don't want some county health inspector breathing down my neck."

"Don't worry, Madge. I remember our little chat from yesterday. No chili sauce. I'm working on something else."

"That's wonderful, honey, but don't do it on salon time, okay?"

"Whatever."

I walked back to my nail station and stacked my empty pickle jars on the floor.

"What's with those smelly looking things?" Trudy asked.

"Oh, I'm filling them with grandma's famous chili sauce tonight and will sell them to our clients. Why not? Helen's selling her stuff here."

Trudy dropped her nail file and ran up front. I love driving her crazy. And thank goodness, Trudy didn't say anything about me being her on TV last night. She was likely too busy fixing her husband's dinner and didn't pay attention to the news.

My first client wasn't due until 10:30, so after preparing my nail station, I decided to wash a load of towels in the storage room. We use them for our pedicures. It also would give me the chance to work on my donation jars. I know Madge told me not during working hours, but she and Helen would be too busy unpacking boxes to notice me. I was still washing the inside of Ritchie's jars when someone knocked on the storage room door.

"Open up, it's the police."

Huh? How could that be? I just talked to Dan a half hour ago.

"The door is open," I replied. "Come in"

A second later, Barton County Sheriff J.D. Pickle strutted through the doorway. He was a pudgy little man about the same size as Mary Donovan and Nate Sloan. The white cowboy hat he wore was too big for his head. It tended to rest on his eyebrows. John Wayne, he's not.

"Are you Candi DeCarlo?" he asked in a gruff-sounding lawman's voice.

"Yessir, what can I do for you? Need a manicure?"

"Don't you go getting cute with me, Missy," he replied. "I'm Barton County Sheriff J.D. Pickle. What were you doing in my jail last night?"

"Visiting my friend, Sylvia Wilson."

"I already know that, or I wouldn't have asked you that question," he said. "What did the two of you talk about?"

"That's privileged information," I said, remembering a phrase I once heard an attorney use on a *Law & Order* rerun.

"You're not a lawyer," he replied, raising his squeaky voice. "You can't use that line on me. I'm the county sheriff, remember. You've got to tell me what you said to her."

"No, I don't."

"Yes, you do."

"No, I don't."

Madge stuck her head in the storage room. "What's all the commotion in here?" she asked. "J.D., why are you harassing my employee? Your shouting is also disturbing my clients."

"I'm not harassing your employee or your clients. I'm the county sheriff, if you haven't forgotten, Madge. I was simply asking Missy, here, a simple question. I want to know what she and Sylvia Wilson talked about in my jail last night."

"What were you doing at his jail last night, Candi?"

"I guess you haven't seen the paper yet," I replied. "Sylvia was arrested yesterday for the murder of Walter Morgan. I felt sorry for her, so I drove over to the jail last night to offer her some moral support."

"Satisfied, J.D.?" Madge asked.

"No, and if I find your employee within fifty feet of my jail again, I'll lock her up and throw away the key."

"You've made your point, J.D," Madge said. "Now, please leave or I'll call the town police and have you removed for trespassing in my nail salon."

"Well, I never…" Sheriff Pickle spouted as he stepped past Madge and left, muttering to himself.

"Sheriff Pickle suffers from a small man complex," Madge said after he'd left. "Hurry up and finish the laundry. Your 10:30 will be here any minute."

It's nice when your employer has your back. Thanks for standing up for me, Madge.

Forty-five minutes later, after I finished with my client, I spotted Nate Sloan carrying an armful of boxes into the salon.

"Watcha got there?" I shouted as he stacked them on the front counter.

"They're Mom's aromatherapy candles. She's started selling them in addition to her cosmetics line."

Darn, this place is turning into a flea market.

I asked Nate to follow me back to my nail station, out of earshot of Madge and his mother. When no one could hear us, I asked, "So, what's the latest with Walter Morgan's murder investigation?"

"You tell me. I heard you met Sylvia Wilson at the county jail last night. Somebody also mentioned they saw you on TV. What's going on?"

"Yeah, I did an interview with Action News. Did Dan tell you I was at the jail?"

"No, I dropped by the station before coming here. The office was all abuzz. Apparently, Chief Cobb called Mary at home this morning and reamed her out."

"I hope I didn't get her in trouble."

"Naw," Nate said. "Mary's used to taking charge of situations. Our old chief would sit in his office all day, feet propped up on his desk, drinking coffee and taking afternoon naps. Mary did all of his paperwork. She needs to realize our new chief is different. He knows what he's doing."

"I hope Mary doesn't get fired," I said, recalling her *Soldier of Fortune* magazine.

"Don't worry. That won't happen," Nate said. "The Chief might put a written reprimand in her personnel file, but that's all. He'll never find anyone willing to work the hours Mary does for the slave wages she receives. So, what *did* you and Sylvia talk about?"

"How she didn't see Walter Monday night and didn't murder him."

"That's funny. She told me and Frank Turner the same story when we picked her up yesterday afternoon. She said Walter called her Monday afternoon and canceled their five o'clock appointment. But I hear Chief Cobb found some incriminating evidence on Walter's desk. It suggests Sylvia murdered Walter to cover up another crime."

"Another crime?" I said. "How could she do that if she didn't meet Walter to talk about the first crime?"

"I dunno," Nate said, scratching his buzz cut. "Maybe she was lying about the phone call. All I know is that it doesn't look good for her."

"What's going to happen to her now?"

"She was formally arraigned on the murder charge an hour ago, with bail set at one million dollars. If she can't make bail, she'll sit in jail until her preliminary hearing. It could take place in a month or longer, depending on Judge Stone's schedule."

"That's not fair. She didn't do it."

"Maybe so, but that's the law. It seems unfair, but who has ten percent of a million bucks to bail themselves out of jail? Listen, I'd better get some sleep before my evening shift begins. It will be a busy night. The carnival people are arriving this afternoon to set up their rides."

"Get some rest," I said, walking Nate to the front door. I also wanted to check on Madge and Helen and their mess.

"Bye, Mom," Nate said as he headed for the front door.

"Nathan, come here and give Mommy a goodbye kiss."

"Do I have to?" Nate asked, his face now bright red.

"I guess not. Go home and get some sleep. Mommy left you a meatloaf dinner in the fridge. Eat it when you wake up. Put it in the microwave for two-and-a-half minutes and it should be fine."

Nate shrugged and made a hasty retreat.

Wow. I didn't think Nate still lived at home. I guess some guys can't handle moving away from their mommies.

"Hey, you, standing over there," Helen barked. "Hand me one of those boxes on the counter, will you?"

Hey you? My name's Candi.

I picked up a box. It weighed a ton. But, I managed to carry it over to Helen.

"Where do you want it?" I asked.

"Let me see," she said, pausing to figure out where I should put the box.

"Can you hurry it up? This box is heavy."

"Aren't we impertinent? Put it down gently at your feet. You can move it later."

I dropped the box on the floor and stomped back to my nail station.

"What's the matter, Candi?" Trudy asked. She could tell I was mad as a hornet. She'd seen that look before. Usually, it was directed at her.

"Helen's already bossing me around. Who does she think she is, anyway?"

"Maybe Helen feels she can tell us what to do now that she's paying Madge rent money."

"I've got news for her. I'm not her slave."

CHAPTER 14

After taking care of my 10:30 client, I told Madge and Helen I was taking an early lunch. They were still busy unpacking boxes. I hoped Helen didn't have too many more, or our poor clients wouldn't have a place to sit.

"Don't take too long," Madge said, poking her head out a large box on the floor. "There'll be lots to do once my nephew and his friend get here."

"Sure thing," I said, opening the front door. I wasn't looking forward to this afternoon. What will our clients think of all this mess? They'd probably want us committed to the loony bin.

My plan was to stop by the bank first to see why Jane Parker had called me at home last night. But, first, I wanted to drop off the two plastic jars in my hands. I had taped a cute sign on the outside of each jar asking people to donate to Sylvia's legal defense fund.

While walking along the east side of the town square, I spotted Johnny Edwards.

"Hey, Mister Private Detective, how's it going?" I asked.

Rather than answer my question, he asked one of his own. "What's with the plastic jars?"

"They're for Sylvia Wilson's legal defense fund. I'm raising money so she can hire a good defense lawyer when she goes on trial for murdering Walter Morgan."

"Yeah, I heard the cops think she did it," Johnny said. "Sorry, I don't have any extra money. Is there another way I can help? Sylvia is such a great lady. She lets me hang out at the Youth Center whenever it rains or it's too cold for me to ride around in my wheelchair."

That's when it hit me. Last night, Sylvia wrote down the businesses she had visited on Tuesday to drop off a poster for the Youth Center's fundraiser on Saturday night. I promised to contact the businesses to learn who may have dropped the nail polish bottle in her purse. The trouble was I didn't have any time now that I was busy working on her legal defense jars.

I reached into my jacket pocket and dug out Sylvia's list and handed it to Johnny. I asked him if he could check on the businesses to see if anyone handed her a bottle of nail polish.

"What exactly does that have to do with Sylvia being a murder suspect?" he asked.

"I'll explain it to you at another time, Johnny. It's a long story, but I've got to drop off these jars and get back to work.

Just see if the store owners remember anything unusual about Sylvia's visit."

"My first investigative job," Johnny said, a big smile forming on his face. "I'll let you know what I find out."

As Johnny wheeled himself down the street, I stepped inside Bowers' Men's Wear. It's next door to the Youth Center. My daughter's high school sweetheart, Wade Bowers, was busy stocking some dress shirts on a shelf at the rear of the store.

"Hi, Wade," I said, approaching him.

He obviously hadn't heard me walk in because he dropped the dress shirts he was holding in his hands.

"Oh hi, Mrs. DeCarlo," he said, reaching for the shirts that fell on the floor. "It's…you. I mean I wasn't expecting you."

"Sorry, I didn't mean to frighten you," I said, bending down to help him pick up the packages of shirts.

"How can I help you today?" he asked.

I told him how I was raising money for Sylvia Wilson's legal defense and asked if I could leave a donation jar on his front counter.

"I heard about the murder," he said, leaning against the shirt counter. "I can't believe Sylvia did it. She seemed so sweet when me and my friends played basketball at the Center."

"Wade, you don't understand," I said, putting on my best version of a stern face. "Sylvia didn't murder Walter Morgan. She's innocent. Do you hear me?"

"Yes, ma'am. Sorry about that. It should be okay to leave one of your donation jars. My dad isn't here right now. He went home for lunch. If he doesn't want to participate, I'll bring it back to you at the nail salon."

"Fair enough."

I handed Wade a jar and was about to leave when he asked, "How's Jenny doing?"

"She's fine," I replied. "And my grandbabies are terrific."

Wade lowered his head. I could tell he still had feelings for Jenny. And, why not? She's a terrific mother. Better than I ever was. I wish her hubby, Andy, wasn't so bull-headed at times. He reminds me too much of my ex.

As I was leaving, I nearly bumped into Town President Douglas Drake. He was standing in the doorway admiring a beige cashmere sports coat draped over a mannequin in the store's display window.

"Well… if it isn't Candi DeCarlo. Fancy meeting you here," he said, with a big smirk on his round face. "Buying a gift for a gentlemen friend?"

Dougie Drake is such a jerk. He must know perfectly well that I don't have a boyfriend. I haven't dated anyone since I divorced Bobby more than two years ago. But Dougie can't help himself. He loves to pick on people. Especially anyone who isn't as rich or as famous as he is. He did it all the time when we were in the high school drama club together.

"No, I'm not buying anyone a gift," I said, looking him straight in the eye. "I dropped off one of my donation jars."

"Huh?"

"Yeah, I'm collecting money for Sylvia Wilson's legal defense fund," I said, poking him in his bulging stomach with my other jar. "Want to donate?"

"What?" he said, glaring at it. "Why are you doing that? Everybody in town knows Sylvia Wilson murdered Walter Morgan. It was in the newspaper this morning."

"Shows you how much you know," I said. "Besides, you shouldn't believe everything you read in the paper."

"What does that mean?" Dougie asked with a perplexed look on his face.

"I talked to Sylvia last night at the county jail."

"But I thought nobody but family members could see her. That's what Chief Cobb told me."

"What can I say?"

I thought Dougie was going to fall over at my news. His complexion was an unflattering shade of fuchsia.

"Are you okay, Dougie?" I asked.

He quickly recovered and walked away without saying goodbye.

Boy, Dougie still hasn't learned any manners.

CHAPTER 15

"Where's Madge and Helen?" I asked Trudy after leaving my other donation jar at Ralph's Diner. I had run out of time to stop by the bank to see why Jane Parker called me at home last night. I would catch up with her later.

"Madge and Helen took a lunch break," Trudy replied. "Last time I saw them they were making a beeline for Pete's Bar. That was more than a half hour ago."

"Pete's for lunch? He doesn't serve food."

"Whatever. They also said something about having a drink to celebrate their new partnership."

"Great, drinking on the job. And where's Madge's nephew? I thought he was going to begin painting this afternoon."

"He called fifteen minutes ago. Said he couldn't hitch a ride from Bloomington. Something about his driver's license being suspended. However, he promised to show up tomorrow."

"Good, at least the salon won't be any messier than it already is. By the way, what if someone drops by and wants to buy some of Helen's cosmetics or a candle? Does she have a price list somewhere?"

"I don't know," Trudy replied, throwing both arms in the air. "I only work here."

"Ain't that the truth?"

"But Madge did tell me one thing before she left."

"What?"

"I can sell my crochet work in the salon if I want. Maybe, you should talk to her again about selling jars of your grandma's famous chili sauce."

"I'm not selling any chili sauce. It was all a big joke. I don't know how to make the stuff. Grandma didn't leave me her recipe before she passed away. I'm using the jars to raise money for Sylvia Wilson."

"That's awfully nice of you, Candi. Sylvia seems like such a nice lady. But, maybe you should check on Madge and Helen. I'm beginning to worry about them."

"Good idea."

Trudy still hadn't said anything about my posing as her on TV last night. She must not have seen the news. That's a good thing. And I certainly wasn't going to tell her.

"I'll be back shortly. Mary Donovan's stopping by at three-thirty."

I grabbed the last plastic jar I had prepared in the storage room before I headed for Pete's Bar on the west side of the town square.

The minute I walked in, I heard them. Madge and Helen. Laughing and talking loudly. But it took a few seconds for my eyes to adjust to the darkness before I figured out where they were sitting.

"Hey, Candi," said Pete Baker. He spotted me first as I made my way to the bar. "Long time no see. Want a drink?"

"No, Pete. I'm still on duty."

"Candi?" Madge said as she swiveled around on her bar stool. "What are you doing here? Did the salon burn down? I knew it. Helen's candles started the fire, right?"

"Oh, sweetheart, that's so funny." Helen laughed and slapped Madge on her back.

They then clicked their glasses and downed their drinks in a single gulp. Judging by the dainty little parasols next to Madge's bar napkin, this wasn't their first or second round.

"The salon hasn't burned down," I said. "Trudy and I were worried that something happened to you."

"Isn't that so sweet, Madge?" said Helen, who appeared ready to fall off her barstool. "Your two girls worrying about you like that."

"They're really wonderful girls, aren't they?" Madge said. "I wouldn't trade them for ten little pigs."

"Ten little pigs? That's so funny, Madge. Stop it, or I'm going to wet my panties. Ten little pigs. Hey, Pete, did you hear that? Ten little pigs. While you're at it, how about a couple more drinks?"

Pete glanced at me and rolled his eyes before stepping away to fix two more fizzy pink drinks.

"Are you coming back to work, Madge?" I asked.

"I don't think so, hon. Have Trudy close the salon. You can leave early if you'd like. You probably don't have another client anyway."

"Actually, I do," I said, glancing at my watch. I still had a half hour before Mary Donovan showed up.

"Whatever," she replied. "Then, you two girls can flip a coin. Loser takes the night deposit to the bank. I'll see you bright and early tomorrow. Now, Helen, want to chug this drink, too?"

I motioned for Pete to follow me to the end of his bar, so I could ask him if he'd take my donation jar.

"Sure thing," he said when I finished my spiel. "Sylvia's a great gal. She lets kids play basketball at the Youth Center all the time. It means they aren't coming in here using fake IDs trying to buy a drink."

"Thanks, Pete."

"Saw you on TV last night," Pete said. "Why didn't you use your own name?"

"It's a long story. I'll tell you another day. I have a client in a few minutes. By the way, I'd cut those two off if I were you."

"Already have. Their last drink was mostly pink lemonade."

As I stepped back onto the street, I spotted a police cruiser parked next to my truck in front of Tips & Toes. Now what? The last thing I needed was another parking ticket. I still hadn't paid the ones stuffed in my glove compartment. I picked up my pace.

"What's up, officer?" I asked, approaching the rear of my truck.

"Didn't you get the word, Candi?" Frank Turner said in greeting me. "Vehicles need to be off the square by three, so the carnival folks can set up their rides."

I glanced at my watch. It was quarter after three.

"Where's your partner?"

"Nate went inside to look for you, but obviously you're not in there because you're out here talking to me."

Frank's power of deduction never fails to amaze me. I jumped into my truck and backed out of the parking spot.

"Leave it behind the building or on one of the side streets," Frank shouted. "Just get it off the town square."

I drove around the corner, found an empty parking spot behind the nail salon, unlocked the back door, and stepped inside. As I emerged from the storage room, I heard Nate and Trudy talking.

"I'm back," I said.

"Where's Madge and Helen?" Trudy asked. "Why didn't you bring them back with you?"

I was all set to say they were drunk on their butts at Pete's but caught myself. I wasn't sure if Nate knew his mommy drank.

"They're having a long conversation with Pete Baker about the future of the businesses on the town square. They won't be back. Madge wants you to close tonight and prepare the night deposit."

"She does? Madge never lets me handle the night deposit. She says I need to hurry home to fix Keith's dinner. Since you don't have a husband, Madge says, there's no reason for you to get home early."

"Is that right?"

Trudy's remark ticked me off. I had half a notion to march back to Pete's and give Madge a piece of my mind, but I decided against it. I'd wait until tomorrow morning when Madge showed up hungover before I got in her face.

"So, Mom's fallen off the wagon again?"

"Nate, I didn't realize she drank. Your mother doesn't seem like the type. I figured Madge must have talked her into it."

"More like the other way around," Nate said. "Mom started drinking like a fish after daddy died a few years back. Her doctor told her it wasn't good for her health, but she didn't listen to him. I'd better go round her up and take her and Madge home."

"Don't say I squealed on them. I don't want them mad at me."

Nate left by the front door. A minute later, Mary Donovan walked in.

"Afternoon, ladies," she said, glancing at Helen's tables. "Am I in the right place? This looks more like a flea market than a nail salon."

"It's all Helen Sloan's stuff," I said.

"Ha, that's a good one," Mary said, slapping her thigh. "Helen has finally pulled one over on somebody. I can't believe Madge bought all this stuff."

"She didn't," I replied. "Helen is renting space from Madge."

"That won't last long," Mary said, as she approached my nail station. "Helen hasn't sold any cosmetics in years. She hates going door to door. Claims she suffers from restless leg syndrome. But she might have better luck with the candles. They at least smell nice."

Mary sat down, and I proceeded to soften her cuticles before working my magic.

"Mary, I'm sorry if I got you in trouble with Dan over what you did for me last night," I said. "I ran into him this morning and he seemed pretty upset with you."

"Don't worry, kiddo. He'll get over it. I need to realize he's brighter than the other chiefs I've worked for, and doesn't need my help like they did."

"But he does need you, Mary," I said, as I began filing the nails on her left hand. "He's got it all wrong about Sylvia."

"What do you mean?"

I told Mary how Sylvia was allergic to nail polish. The polish Dan found in her purse wasn't hers.

"I hadn't heard about the nail polish," Mary said when I finished. "The Chief isn't as chatty as the last chief. That changes everything, doesn't it?"

"Yes, and Nate told me something else this morning when he dropped off some of his mom's stuff."

"What was that?"

"When Nate and Frank picked up Sylvia yesterday, she said Walter had called her and canceled their scheduled meeting on Monday afternoon. She was never in his office."

"I hadn't heard that story, either. Darn, I must be losing my touch."

"No, it's like you said earlier. Sylvia's comments have changed everything. That's why I've started a legal defense fund for her. But I'm still worried about her. Sylvia said Dan found a folder with some incriminating evidence in it on Walter's desk. Know what that was about?"

"I have no idea. As I said before, the Chief has been very secretive about Sylvia's arrest."

"Well, I believe she's being railroaded, but I don't know who's behind it."

"It definitely sounds like it. How can I help?"

"You can start by telling Dan what I've told you about the nail polish and Sylvia's canceled meeting with Walter. Maybe, you can talk some sense into that handsome head of his."

"I'll do what I can, but he's plenty mad at me right now. I thought he'd fire me this morning."

"Don't get yourself fired, Mary. Just see what you can do. By the way, how did you persuade that jail guard to let me see Sylvia?"

"It's a long story," Mary said. "Dexter McIntyre once worked for us, but he was a lazy cop. Never wrote up his reports. I did them for him until I became sick and was off work for a whole week. The Chief at the time figured out what was happening and fired him.

"In the meantime, Candi, keep nosing around to see who uses that nail polish you mentioned. How much do I owe you today?"

"Don't worry about it. It's on the house."

"But, won't Madge find out?"

"In Madge's present condition, she'll be lucky if she can remember her own name."

CHAPTER 16

"Got any more clients?" I asked Trudy after Mary Donovan left.

"Nope, my last client wanted a set of acrylics. She left an hour ago."

"Then, let's close up early and go home."

"But, what if Madge and Helen come back? You know how Madge is about closing the salon early."

"I know, but don't worry. They won't be back. Besides, Nate has probably already driven them home. They were in no shape to come back to work. And, this way, you can go home early and work on your crochet pieces."

"Great idea, Candi. You don't mind? After all, you said Madge wanted me to drop off the night deposit tonight."

"Don't worry. I'll take care of it. I usually do. Remember, I don't have a husband at home waiting for me."

Trudy gave me a big grin before she grabbed her blue University of Kentucky hoodie off the coat rack at the rear of the salon and left through the back door. Good. She still hadn't mentioned anything about last night's TV interview. Trudy obviously hadn't seen it. And apparently, none of her clients had said anything to her. I wondered what they talked about.

It took me less than five minutes to pull together the night deposit, turn off the lights, lock the front door, and drive to the bank. All I wanted to do now was go home and forget everything that happened today. A nice warm bath and a large glass of Diet Dr. Pepper would do the trick.

A half hour later, I felt myself nodding off in my tub when I heard the kitchen phone ring. I ignored it. It was probably a telemarketer trying to persuade me to buy something I didn't need. I climbed out of the tub a few minutes later, dried off, grabbed my bathrobe, and wandered into the kitchen to see if the caller had left a message.

"It's me," Mandy's recorded voice on the machine announced. "Get ready. I'm picking you up at seven. We're going to Walter's wake."

Why did Mandy want to go there? She hated Walter Morgan. All those nasty things she said about him on Monday night after she picked me up at the police station. What had changed her mind?

The clock on my microwave read 6:50 p.m. Darn, Mandy would be here any minute, and I'm not dressed. I rushed into the bedroom and opened my closet door. What do people wear to a wake? Black, right?

I pulled out my black miniskirt, but it was badly wrinkled. I didn't have time to iron it. I'll have to wear a pair of black jeans and my lacey black bustier instead.

I had just grabbed my fur coat from the front closet when I heard someone on the street laying on their car horn. It was probably Mandy. She hates climbing the twenty-plus steps to my apartment's front door. Says it makes her sweat and messes up her makeup. Instead, Mandy blasts her horn whenever she stops by.

I ran downstairs to Mandy's car and jumped inside.

"Why are we going to Walter's wake?" I asked, while buckling my seat belt.

"I don't know," Mandy replied. "It might be fun to see who shows up to pay their respects to the old coot. Besides, I have a big tire sale starting tomorrow and won't have time to attend his funeral."

"Think the killer will be there?"

"Huh?"

"I once saw an episode of *Law & Order* where the bad guy revisited the scene of the crime. Maybe, the murderer will show up tonight to make sure Walter's dead."

"If he does, he'll likely receive a standing ovation," Mandy said, as she maneuvered her Jaguar into the crowded parking lot at Carson Brothers Funeral Home, the largest funeral home in Barton County.

"Can't I wait out here for you?" I asked Mandy as she brought her car to a stop. "This place gives me the willies. The last time I was here was when we buried Grandma Thompson. It took me a week to get over it."

"No, you can't sit here by yourself. Now, come on, let's get this over with so I can go home and take a nice long bubble bath."

A tall, skinny guy dressed in a charcoal gray suit greeted us as we walked inside the funeral home. He insisted on us signing a guest book sitting on a wobbly wooden podium to his left. What was up with that? Does some town official go through the names later to record who showed up and who didn't? Once we scrawled our names, the guy said we could hang up our coats on a portable coat rack a few feet away.

"You're not wearing that inside, are you?" Mandy said after I took off my coat and hung it up. She started shaking her head side to side.

"What's wrong?"

"It's your outfit. This is a funeral home, not Ray's Hideaway Lounge," she said, quickly removing her stunning black blazer and handing it to me. "Put this on."

"Thanks, I guess."

"Can you believe this crowd?" Mandy asked after we walked into the viewing room. We took our place in the long line to the right of Walter's casket.

"It's nice so many people showed up to pay their respects," I said. "It shows how important Walter was to everyone in Bartonsville. I'm certainly going to miss him."

"Yeah, right, but I know why you'll miss him," Mandy whispered in my ear. "His tips. But I bet if you took a poll among everyone here, you'd find the majority came tonight to make sure the old coot is dead. Most business owners I know truly hated him."

Mandy and I slowly inched along the line until we were next to view Walter. I took a deep breath before glancing down at him. His head was resting on a white satin pillow. He looked the same way he did on Monday night. He was wearing a gray banker's suit, a white shirt, and a black tie. I hoped it wasn't the same suit he was wearing when he was stabbed. There'd be a big hole in the back of it. The only difference I noticed tonight was that his eyes were shut, and his hands were neatly folded in front of him.

Hmmm?

I wondered if the Carson brothers had removed the pink nail polish from his nails.

As Mandy and I moved past the casket, she asked, "Did you see any pink nail polish?"

"Nope, they must have removed it," I said. "So, can we go now?"

"It's not polite to leave right away. Let's stand against that far wall for a few minutes. We can watch the expression on people's faces as they look at Walter. Who knows? Somebody may spit in his eye."

Sometimes, I'm embarrassed at how crude Mandy can be. It's a holdover from her days as a biker momma.

As Mandy and I stood there, Lonnie Sparks yelled across the room at me.

"All of my friends love my new French nails, Candi. Some of them may call you."

Everyone in line turned and stared at me. I grabbed Mandy's blazer and pulled it tight around me.

"Are you the young woman who found Walter?"

I looked to my right. Irene Morgan was standing in front of me and Mandy.

"Yes, I was in the bank on Monday night," I said. "I'm truly sorry for your loss."

"Thank you," Mrs. Morgan said. "I know you're about to leave, but I wonder if you could do me a favor. I'd like to talk to you privately about Walter. Perhaps you could drop by the house later."

I looked at Mandy. She had the same surprised look on her face I had. Finally, I spoke up.

"Sure."

"Fine," Mrs. Morgan said, patting my arm. "I should be home in an hour or so."

Once outside the funeral home, I asked Mandy. "What was that all about?"

"Beats me," she replied. "Maybe Irene has some bizarre notion that you and Walter were having an affair."

"Yuck. You can't be serious."

CHAPTER 17

The Morgan house sits in the middle of a block on State Street. It's a traditional, two-story, white colonial with green shutters. One of the finest-looking homes on that street or, for that matter, in the entire town. When Mandy and I were in elementary school, we'd have sleepovers at her house. Her parents' place was around the corner and much smaller.

We often would walk past the Morgan house and stare at it, daydreaming of the day when we'd live in a mansion like that. Mandy's wish came true when Marvin built her a palace on the edge of town. Me? I'm still waiting for my Prince Charming to show up with his hammer and nails.

As I approached the front steps, I wondered again why Mrs. Morgan asked to see me in private. Was Mandy right? Did Mrs. Morgan think I was having an affair with Walter?

Mandy and I tossed around a few other theories after leaving the funeral home, but the affair kept coming back to us. It didn't make any sense. Mandy made me pinky promise to call her the minute I left Mrs. Morgan's house and fill her in on all the gory details of my visit.

I rang the doorbell. A minute passed before Mrs. Morgan opened her front door. She had removed the black dress she had worn at the funeral home, and was wearing a pale pink housecoat and matching slippers. She looked frail. That was understandable. I couldn't imagine what it would be like to lose your husband. I remember how emotionally upset I was when I lost Bobby, but that was different. He moved out to live fulltime with one of his skanky girlfriends.

"Oh, Miz DeCarlo, you've come," she said, sounding surprised to see me.

Duh? Hadn't she invited me? Or, had she already forgotten?

Mrs. Morgan opened the door wider, so I could enter the foyer and follow her into the living room. It was gorgeous. Better than anything I'd imagined when Mandy and I had stood outside her house as kids. The room featured dark mahogany crown molding. An enormous brown brick fireplace filled the far wall. A huge, old-fashioned celery green sofa and several straight back chairs were tastefully arranged about the room. Too formal for my taste. I'm more into country chic, but I sat down in one of her chairs anyway.

"May I get you something to drink?" Mrs. Morgan asked. "Perhaps a cup of tea?"

"Ah…no, I don't think so, but thanks for asking."

Mrs. Morgan must have sensed I wasn't a big tea drinker. Diet Dr. Pepper. Now, that's a different story.

"How about something a little stronger?" she asked, walking over to the large China cabinet in the far corner of the room. She reached inside and pulled out a liquor bottle. "I'll be right back."

While she was gone, I took off my fur jacket and studied the room more closely. It was bigger than my entire apartment. I could get used to living in a place like this, but that wasn't going to happen unless I won the Hoosier Lottery or met my dream carpenter.

"Here you go, dear," Mrs. Morgan said, handing me a tall glass tumbler upon her return.

I wasn't sure what was in the glass, but wanting to be polite, I took a sip. Whoa. Straight vodka. I hadn't had a drink that potent in years. Already I could feel it curling my hair.

Mrs. Morgan sat down in a matching straight back chair on the other side of the room. She took a big swig of her drink before placing it on the table next to her chair.

"I like your outfit," she said.

"They were the only black clothes I could find in my closet, except for my black miniskirt."

"It's very provocative," Mrs. Morgan said, taking another gulp of her drink. "Do you always wear clothes like that?"

Poor Mrs. Morgan. I could tell she was working up the courage to ask me if I'd been having an affair with Walter. I decided to put her mind at ease.

"In case you're wondering, I went to the bank on Monday night because Walter missed his appointment. I've been taking care of his hangnail problem for the past three months. Our relationship was strictly professional. Nothing else was going on between us."

"A nail appointment?"

"Yes," I replied, explaining again how I'd been treating her husband's hangnails.

"Interesting," she said when I finished. "Walter never mentioned any nail appointments. When I asked where he went on Monday nights, he said something about a service club meeting." She took another swig of her drink. "But that helps to explain certain things."

"Certain things?"

"Yes, dear, Walter has been more preoccupied than normal in the past few months. I couldn't figure out why. At first, I thought it was me. You know. Maybe he was unhappy with the meals I fixed for him, or maybe I wasn't putting enough starch in his undershirts. But, after listening to you, other things have become more clear. I need to show you something. Mind coming upstairs with me? But first, I need a refill."

I wasn't sure what Mrs. Morgan wanted to show me, but I decided to go along with her in hopes of finding a clue about Walter's murder. I patiently waited for her to return with a fresh drink. One thing was certain. This frail-looking little woman could drink. I followed her up the winding staircase to her master bedroom.

"Still there, dear?" Mrs. Morgan asked. "It's in our walk-in closet. By the way, you can call me Irene if you'd like. That's my first name."

"Okay, Irene," I said. "And you can call me Candi."

Irene stepped into her closet and came out a moment later holding a beautiful turquoise sequined gown.

"That's gorgeous, Irene. Where did you get it?"

"I didn't. It belongs to Walter."

"What?" I replied. "It's Walter's dress?"

"Yes," Irene said, letting the gown slowly fall to the floor while she took another sip of her drink. "I found it in the corner of his closet on Tuesday morning while looking for a gray suit to give to the funeral home people. I figured Walter probably bought it for his girlfriend. But, I can see now that it's too big for you."

I was lost for words.

"I know what you're probably thinking, Candi," Irene said. "Walter was a philanderer. I don't want to believe it, either. We had a loving relationship over the years, but lately, he's been less attentive if you know what I mean. I figured he was simply too busy with his work and didn't have time for me. Now, I don't know what to think."

As I tried to figure out what to say next, I noticed that Irene was now gently swaying back and forth in the middle of the bedroom.

"I'm feeling a little light-headed," she said softly.

Irene was ready to fall on the floor at any second. I rushed over and carefully steered her towards her bed. She sat down on the side of it.

"Thank you, dear. I must be tired. I hope you don't mind if I lie down for a minute."

Irene keeled over on her pillow. I quickly removed the drink clutched in her hand. No sense spilling it on her expensive-looking bedspread. I put the drink on the nightstand before reaching down and removing Irene's slippers. I then pulled her feet up on the bed. Within a minute, she was softly snoring. I pulled the blue blanket lying at the foot of the bed over her to keep her warm. She seemed okay, so I figured it would be all right to leave her alone. She simply needed to sleep off the booze.

I was about to leave her bedroom when I wondered if there were other evening gowns in Walter's closet. Why not take a quick peek? I'd be careful and wouldn't disturb anything. I picked up the turquoise sequined gown off the floor.

Walter's charcoal gray banker's suits were arranged on the right side of the walk-in closet. No doubt, one for each day of the week. Same for his multiple pairs of black shoes. The man had more shoes than most women I know. A tiny box lay on the floor next to them. I got down on my hands and knees to take a closer look. The box resembled an old fishing tackle box. I pulled it towards me and opened it.

"What's Walter doing with a tackle box full of makeup?" I asked, although Irene was in no condition to answer me.

That was too weird. I quickly put the tackle box away and checked on Irene to make sure she was still sleeping soundly before leaving her house. Once on her front sidewalk, I pulled out my cell phone and called Mandy.

"You'll never guess what I found inside Irene's house," I shouted after Mandy picked up.

"Go ahead. Try me."

"Walter had a turquoise sequined gown in his closet."

"Huh?"

"It gets better. I also found a tackle box full of makeup next to his shoes."

"Pink nails? Turquoise sequined gown? Makeup. My Gawd, was Walter a cross-dresser?"

"It looks like it," I said. "Don't that beat all?"

"Sure does," Mandy sighed. "If only I had known."

I'd heard enough about Mandy's feelings for Walter on Monday night. I didn't want her going down that path again, so I quickly changed the subject.

"Did your friend Carol have any more news about Sylvia?"

"Yeah, I talked to her an hour ago. Sylvia isn't doing well. She's depressed and doesn't know where she'll get the money for a lawyer to defend her when her trial begins."

"I was afraid you'd say that," I said. "Looks like I'll be making more donation jars pronto. After all, it's not like I had anything else to do."

CHAPTER 18

"Another rough night?" Joanie asked after dropping a medium Diet Dr. Pepper and cinnamon swirl in front of me on Thursday morning.

"Rough doesn't begin to describe it," I grunted.

"So, let's hear all about it," Joanie said, as she bent over and rested her elbows on the lunch counter.

I took a quick swig of my drink and told her about meeting Irene Morgan at her house last night and learning that Walter had a turquoise sequined gown hanging in his closet.

"A cross-dresser, eh?" Joanie said when I finished. "Never figured that old fuddy-duddy liked women's clothes. People think I'm weird because I have a live-in girlfriend."

"Walter wasn't like that," I said, gently scolding Joanie. "I didn't see any other outfits in his closet. But I did also find a tackle box full of makeup. I don't know what to think anymore."

"Straight people never cease to amaze me," Joanie sighed. "I can never figure them out."

"I don't know about that, but something's definitely screwy here, and I need to find out what it is."

"Knock yourself out, Candi."

Joanie picked up a carafe from the back counter and wandered off to refill the coffee mugs of her customers.

Right. Knock yourself out, Candi. I said to myself as I continued munching on my cinnamon swirl. After a minute or so of contemplation, I recalled my brief conversation with Sylvia Wilson on Tuesday morning.

Of course, that's it. The faux beauty pageant on Saturday night. Sylvia handed me a poster to put in the salon's front window. I bet Walter intended to be one of the contestants. But, why? If he was so worried about folks finding out about his hangnail appointments, why risk his reputation by cross-dressing? Then again, perhaps Walter wanted to change his image. Show everyone in town that he was a hip guy by being in the drag show. It could explain the gown and makeup.

"Morning, Candi," Johnny Edwards said as he steered his wheelchair next to the lunch counter.

"What are you up to this morning?"

"Remember, you asked me to check out the list of businesses that Sylvia Wilson gave you on Tuesday night.

"What did you find out?"

"Nothing. Nobody was offering free nail polish samples and none of them remembered seeing any customers doing the same."

Hmmm.

"That bottle didn't just jump into Sylvia's purse. But, thanks for trying, Johnny."

"No problem. Is there anything else I can do to help?"

"As a matter of fact, there is. Did you notice the poster for the faux beauty pageant?"

"Yeah, they're hung up in store windows all around the square."

"Think you can find out who the contestants are?"

"Sure," Johnny said. "I'll do my best, but why are you so interested in the beauty contestants?"

"Just a hunch, but it may have something to do with Walter's murder."

"Really?"

"Yeah, but I can't say anything more right now. Let me know what you find out."

"I'm on it," Johnny said, as he turned his motorized wheelchair around and left the diner.

"What was that all about?" Joanie asked with an empty coffee carafe in her hand.

"I just sent Johnny on a wild goose chase."

I looked at my Betty Boop watch. Time for work. I left my money next to my plate and walked down the street to Tips & Toes.

"Hi, Madge," I said after walking in the front door a few minutes later. "How are you feeling this morning?"

I don't know why I bothered to ask. I could plainly see Madge felt bad. Real bad. She was wearing oversized sunglasses and was holding onto the front counter with both hands as though she was about to fall off her stool.

Madge muttered something in a low voice, but I let it go. No sense carrying on a conversation with her in her present condition. I continued walking back to my nail station.

"Some hangover, huh?"

It was Trudy. She was standing next to my nail station.

"I know how she's feeling," I said. "Been there and done that a few times myself."

"I wouldn't know."

"Right. I forgot. You don't drink, Little Goody Two-Shoes."

I wanted to say that, but instead, I asked Trudy where Helen was.

"She called a few minutes ago. Said she'll try to make it in by noon."

"That's a great way to start her business."

"Madge's nephew, Lenny, and his best friend, Earl, showed up a half hour ago. They started setting up their painting equipment, but Madge sent them home. Said they were making too much noise. Lenny and Earl didn't seem upset. I don't think they're too eager to paint the salon."

At noon, I took a lunch break. It looked as if Madge hadn't moved since I first walked into work. She was still wearing her sunglasses, and her hands hadn't let go of the front counter.

When I got to the diner, a few minutes later, McPherson was slouched in the back booth, munching on his usual cheeseburger deluxe platter.

"Got a minute?" I asked. "I need some information."

"Too cheap to buy a newspaper?" he said, taking a bite of his burger. "Sit down."

"Know anything about the faux beauty pageant on Saturday night?"

"You mean that silly idea that Dougie Drake dreamed up to raise money for the Youth Center? Why are you asking?"

"Oh, I don't know," I replied, motioning for Joanie to bring me a grilled cheese and Diet Dr. Pepper. "I'm just curious about the contest. Who are the contestants? Why would some of our leading citizens embarrass themselves like that in front of everyone? You know how folks in town tend to react to anything out of the ordinary."

"Hmmm," McPherson said, wiping some mustard off his pudgy chin. "I hadn't thought of it that way. Maybe I should find out who the contestants are before Saturday. But, why are you asking me? Know something you're not telling me, Candi?"

"What do you mean?"

"Like, you already know who they are, and you're just messing with me."

"I'd never mess with you, McPherson."

"Right, I remember all the times you nearly spilled drinks on me when you worked here."

"It wasn't my fault. The diner's floors are uneven."

"Whatever," McPherson said before leaning across the table. "Now, come clean. You know one of the contestants, don't you? Tell me who it is."

"I'm not sure," I replied. "But, you need to see what you can find out."

"Great idea," McPherson said as he rubbed his face one last time with a napkin. "But, right now, I have an interview with Chief Cobb. I want to see if he's making any progress on Walter Morgan's murder. I'll check out the contestant list when I get a chance."

McPherson threw his money on the table, slid out of the booth, and promptly left.

A minute later, Joanie stood in front of the booth.

"McPherson didn't leave me a tip again," she said, picking up his money and the dirty dishes he left behind. "How can I retire if he doesn't start leaving me some change?"

"Don't hold your breath," I said, laughing. "He never tipped me either."

"Why was he in such a hurry to leave? Is the courthouse on fire?"

"No, he's interviewing Dan about Walter's murder, but I also put a bug in his ear about Saturday's faux beauty pageant."

"You didn't tell him about Walter's sequined gown, did you?"

"No, I figured he could find out that on his own. He's the reporter, after all. I've got Johnny checking it out as well."

"You're sneaky, Candi."

"Thanks for the compliment."

CHAPTER 19

When I returned to the salon after lunch, Helen was fussing over her table of scented candles.

"Did Madge go home?" I asked.

"No, Trudy and I helped her back to the storage room where she's lying on the table back there."

Ouch! That can't be comfortable.

"How are you feeling?"

"Fine, honey. Can't you tell?"

I had to admit Helen didn't look as bad as Madge did this morning. Hangovers affect everyone differently.

"What happened to you this morning?"

"My darn alarm clock didn't go off. I'll have to stop by Walmart on the way home and buy myself a new one."

"Whatever you say, Helen. I'm going to check on Madge."

I walked past Trudy on my way to the storage room. She was busy painting a client's nails.

When I reached the storage room, I opened the door very slowly. I didn't want to wake Madge if she was sound asleep.

"Candi, help me down off this table," Madge said when she realized I was standing next to her.

She grabbed my arms as she tried to sit up and steady herself before stepping down from the table.

"Whew," she said when her feet finally touched the floor. "I still feel a little woozy. Got any aspirin?"

"I have some at my nail station, but you need something else."

"What are you talking about?"

"How about a quick trip to Pete's for a little hair of the dog?"

"Hair of the dog, huh? Maybe, you're right. One drink couldn't hurt me, could it? I don't want you girls to get the wrong idea about me."

"We don't think badly of you, Madge. We want you to feel better. Now, let's go get you that drink."

Madge and I walked out of the storage room hand in hand and headed for the front door.

"Where are you two going?" Helen asked.

"We're off to Pete's for a drink," I said.

"Can I come?"

"Sure, why not. The more the merrier."

The three of us slowly made our way the half block to Pete Baker's. He was standing behind his bar, washing some glasses and didn't notice us at first. As Helen and I helped Madge up on a bar stool, Pete looked up.

"Well…well…" he said, wiping his hands with the towel next to his glass washer. "Are you ladies looking to become regulars?"

I answered for them.

"No, Madge and Helen simply need a little eye opener and nothing more."

"Doctor Pete has exactly what they need," he said, before grabbing a bottle of Jim Beam off his back counter.

"One drink, ladies. Drink it slowly and then it's back to work," I said, sounding more like a kindergarten teacher than a professional manicurist. "You don't want to end up feeling like you did this morning."

Pete winked at me as I left the bar. I hoped it meant he'd serve Madge and Helen only one drink each.

Trudy was standing in the middle of the nail salon, her arms folded in front of her chest.

What's up with her?

"Trying to turn Madge and Helen into a pair of alcoholics?"

"Trust me. One drink will make them feel a hundred percent better. Wait and see."

As Trudy went back to her nail station, she said someone called me while I was at Pete's.

"Was it my friend, Mandy?"

"No."

"What did the person want?"

"She didn't say. Said she'd call back later."

A few more minutes went by before Madge and Helen walked arm and arm through the front door.

"Where's Candi?" they shouted. "She's a miracle worker."

I looked up and smiled. I was applying some orange-colored nail polish to Peggy Adams, one of my regulars. But that didn't stop Madge and Helen. They strolled back to my nail station.

"Group hug," Madge shouted as she and Helen ordered me to stand up, so they could throw their arms around me.

I was glad they were feeling better, but I knew Peggy Adams was in a hurry. She was anxious to finish getting her booth ready for the Foliage Festival. Peggy makes beautiful outfits for Barbie doll collectors.

Once Madge and Helen were done with their hugs, they went up to the front counter. About fifteen minutes later, Madge shouted for me. Was she needing another group hug?

"It's for you," she said, handing me the phone.

Who could it be?

"Is this Miz DeCarlo?" asked the voice on the other end of the line.

"Yes," I said hesitantly.

"It's Irene Morgan. I found something interesting this morning that you might like to see.Can you drop by after work?"

"Sure."

Maybe Irene found some unmentionables in Walter's sock drawer.

CHAPTER 20

On my way to Irene Morgan's house, I wondered what she had found. Could it be the clue that would solve his murder? If so, why hadn't she called Dan instead? It didn't make any sense. I still didn't believe Walter was a philanderer.

I parked my truck in front of Irene's house and jogged up to her front door and rang the doorbell. A few seconds later, she opened her door.

"Come in, Candi," she said, smiling at me. Irene was wearing a simple A-line black dress with a beautiful pearl necklace. She looked as if she'd been to an afternoon tea with some friends instead of being at her husband's funeral.

Irene and I walked into her living room and sat down. She offered me a cup of coffee, but I politely declined. I was thankful she didn't break open the vodka bottle again. That one drink on my last visit had been more than enough for me. Besides, I wasn't here to help drown her sorrows. I was simply curious to hear what she'd found.

"First of all, please accept my apology for the way I behaved last night," Irene said. "I don't know what overcame me. I'm a God-fearing Christian woman who doesn't normally indulge in evil spirits, at least, not all the time. I feel so ashamed."

"Don't worry," I replied. "It wasn't your fault. You've been under a tremendous amount of stress lately with Walter's murder, the funeral arrangements and everything else. How about if we change the subject? Tell me what you found earlier today."

"Yes, of course," Irene said. "I'm sure you need to rush home and fix dinner for your husband. I won't hold you up. Now, if I could just remember where I left that note."

Irene stood up, looked around her chair as if the note had fallen on the floor before she walked into an adjoining room. She came back a minute later, holding a piece of paper tightly in her right hand.

"I found this on top of Walter's dresser this morning," she said, handing me the folded paper. "I watched him take it out of his suit coat on Monday morning before he left for work. I didn't think anything of it at the time. But, as I was searching for his address book earlier, I found it."

I unfolded the paper and found myself staring at five names. They were the names of some prominent people in town. And, for some reason, Walter's name had been crossed out with a pencil.

"You're probably wondering what those names mean, right?"

I nodded in response to Irene's question.

"I had the same reaction when I first saw the list," Irene said. "But, then I remembered how Walter always wore that same gray suit on Mondays. The note must be a premonition of some kind. You know, like someone put it in an envelope and mailed it to him late last week. It's a warning of some kind, or worse, a death threat. A warning that he would be the first to die."

Premonition? First to die? And, I thought I had an overactive imagination after watching Steven Seagal movies late at night. Sounds like Irene watches the same movies.

Personally, I don't believe in conspiracy theories or any of that psychic mumbo jumbo stuff you hear on cable TV. I once had my fortune read, but the fortune teller wouldn't tell me when Prince Charming would show up on my doorstep. However, I could tell from the expression on Irene's face that she thought the note was important, so I didn't want to upset her.

"I could talk to everyone on the list to see what the note might mean. And, if you're right about it being a premonition or something worse, at least I can warn everyone to be on the lookout for trouble."

"Candi, that would be wonderful. I was going to call Chief Cobb and tell him, but he might think I'm losing my mind. Making a fuss over a simple handwritten list. Besides, he wouldn't have done anything with the note. You, on the other hand…."

Yeah, like I've got nothing better to do than run around town asking about the handwritten note stuffed in the gray suit that Walter always wore on Mondays.

I felt like saying that to Irene, but I couldn't do it. I didn't want to hurt her feelings or leave her more depressed than she already appeared to be. I wasn't sure how much liquor was left in her China cabinet. Like a good girl, I told Irene I'd check out the names and report back to her as soon as possible.

"That would be wonderful, Candi," she gushed. "It will help me sleep better at night, I'm sure."

Irene walked me to her front door, gave me a warm hug, and showed me out. As I drove home, I thought about the significance of Walter's name on the list. I recognized the other names, except for one. Let me see, there was the town president, the publisher of the *Beacon,* the owner of the town's wooden pallet factory, and Salty. I'd never heard of anyone with that nickname. Could it belong to a former Navy commander or maybe a fisherman?"

I should call Mandy. Salty might be a member of the country club. Right now, though, all I wanted was to go home, take a warm bath, and crawl into bed with Freddy. Tomorrow promised to be a busy day with more folks coming to town for the Foliage Festival.

After parking my truck on the street, I climbed the steps to my second-floor apartment. The older I get, I swear the number of steps keep increasing.

I unlocked my front door and stepped inside. That's when something crunched underneath my feet. I switched on the light and looked down. Shards of glass. All over my carpet. Where did they come from? I then noticed a pane of glass in my front door was broken. Oh, my God, somebody has broken into my apartment.

I took another step beyond the doorway. My combination living room and kitchenette was a total mess. Stuff was strewn all over the place. I walked to my stove and pulled out the large cast iron frying pan I keep in the oven. If the burglar was still here, he'd be in for a headache when I was finished with him.

With my trusty frying pan firmly in my right hand, I tiptoed to the door of my spare bedroom and turned on the light. Nobody was there, but someone had opened my chest of drawers. Clothes were strewn all over the place. Next on my tour of destruction was my own bedroom. Same result. Nobody there, but my clothes and Freddy were thrown on the floor.

That left only one more place to check. My bathroom. I noticed the door was slightly ajar. I always keep it closed. Maybe I surprised Mister Burglar Man by coming home early and he was hiding behind the shower curtain, waiting to slice me up with a butcher knife. But I was ready. I was now holding my frying pan in both hands. I walked into the bathroom and switched on the light.

"Come out from behind that curtain, psycho," I shouted.

No response. Mister Burglar Man wasn't there, but he'd left a calling card. Scrawled on the mirror of my medicine cabinet above the sink was this message: "Mind your own business." And Mister Burglar Man had used my favorite new lipstick to write it, no less. Damn him.

I shut off the bathroom light and walked back into the living room when I heard someone turning the knob to my front door. Maybe Mister Burglar Man had come back to finish me off. I'll show him. Wasting my new, expensive lipstick like that. The door swung open. It was Mandy. She was holding some Chinese takeout in her hands.

"What are you doing here?"

"I thought I'd surprise you by dropping by with dinner," she said, quickly surveying the room. "Honey, what's going on?"

"Somebody broke in and left a note on my bathroom mirror."

Mandy rushed over, handed me the bag of takeout food and ran into the bathroom. She rejoined me a few seconds later.

"We're calling the police."

I hoped my second interview with the police would go better than the first.

CHAPTER 21

"Can I talk to you for a minute, Candi?"

I'd taken the last bite of my cinnamon swirl at Ralph's Diner on Friday morning when I heard the deep male voice behind me. It was Dan. I motioned for him to have a seat on the stool next to me.

"I heard about your break-in last night," he said, looking genuinely concerned. "Someone at the station mentioned you usually stop here on your way to work, so I came by to ask you a few questions. Is that okay?"

"Go ahead," I stammered, reaching for my Diet Dr. Pepper to wash down the last of the cinnamon swirl stuck in my throat.

"The report said someone left a message on your bathroom mirror," Dan said, now looking directly at me. "Are you getting in someone's business that you shouldn't?"

I dropped my head and looked at my hands. "I don't think so."

I didn't want to tell Dan about the turquoise sequined gown I saw in Walter's clothes closet or his name on what Irene thinks is a death list.

"Well, that's not exactly what I hear"

"Oh…. What have you heard?"

"You've set up a fund for Sylvia Wilson's legal defense and you've been dropping off donation jars to businesses all around the town square."

"Is that a crime?"

"No, but you may have upset the murderer and any of his accomplices. Whoever killed Walter Morgan wants everyone to think Sylvia Wilson is the guilty party. The last thing they want to see is you helping her to go free."

"Having second thoughts about Sylvia's guilt?"

"Not necessarily. The prosecutor still thinks we have a solid case, but Mary told me about her conversation with you on Wednesday. How Sylvia is apparently allergic to nail polish and how Walter called Sylvia on Monday afternoon and canceled his appointment with her. I'll check out those facts when I meet with her later today."

"Tell me how you knew all about my legal defense fund campaign?"

"It's all over the front page this morning."

"I don't read the paper. The news is too depressing for me."

"Well, you might want to read about it yourself. It looks like McPherson didn't misquote you in his front-page story like he sometimes does with me."

"Bless his big cheeseburger deluxe heart."

I don't know anything about that," Dan said. "But, it's another reason not to get involved in Walter's murder. Whoever killed him means business. Be careful. If you notice anything suspicious, call me. Do you hear me?"

"I promise," I said, raising my right hand. "You'll be the first to know."

Dan nodded before calling Joanie over to the counter.

"How much do I owe you for the coffee?"

"It's on the house, Chief."

Dan gave Joanie a big smile before he stood up and left the diner.

"So, let's hear it," Joanie said as she leaned on the counter. "Tell me everything the two of you talked about. Did he ask you out on a date?"

"No. What makes you think he'd ask me out on a date?"

Joanie grinned. "A little bird told me the Chief seems interested in you."

"More like a big bird with a loose beak," I said. "You shouldn't listen to everything McPherson tells you."

"But, you wouldn't turn down Chief Cobb if he asked you out, would you?"

"Of course not," I replied. "I may be forty-two, but I'm not ready for a nursing home yet. Besides, I recently read a magazine article in which it said that men are most attracted to women my age."

"I wouldn't know anything about that, and frankly I don't care," Joanie offered. "So, if you and the Chief didn't talk about dating, what did you talk about?"

"He wanted to know about the break-in at my apartment last night."

"Break-in? At your apartment? You didn't say anything about a break-in when you first walked in this morning."

"I know. I'm sorry. I was still half asleep. Mandy and I were up until one o'clock putting everything back in its place."

I gave Joanie the *Reader's Digest* version of what happened and how Mandy and I wondered if it had something to do with Walter's murder.

"So, what's the Chief doing about it?"

"He wants me to keep my nose out of Walter's murder investigation."

"Speaking of which, he dropped some money in Sylvia's jar on his way out."

"He did?"

"Yep. Didn't you see him?"

"No, I was too busy looking at the newspaper. I don't remember talking to McPherson about creating donation jars for Sylvia."

"He said he couldn't track you down yesterday, so he asked me what you were doing to help defend her," Joanie said.

"You made me sound like I know what I'm doing. Good quotes. I owe you."

"Glad you feel that way," Joanie said.

"So, what are you hearing from folks about Sylvia? Do they think she murdered Walter?"

"Everyone I've talked to said they love her and what she's done for the kids at the Youth Center. I haven't found anybody who thinks she's guilty."

"That's great to hear."

"By the way, I was bored after the lunch rush yesterday. I sat down and counted the money in the jar. There's nearly sixty bucks there. Want to take it with you?"

"No, leave it there. The more money people see, the more they're likely to donate. I'll pick it up later. I still need to open a bank account for Sylvia."

"Okay but take Chief Cobb's advice and be careful. Next to my Patty, you're the best friend I have. I don't want to see you get hurt."

"I'll be careful," I said as I stood up, gave Joanie a big hug before I left.

CHAPTER 22

On my way to the nail salon, I wondered what today would bring. When I left last night, Madge and Helen were in high spirits. And not the liquid kind. They were reminiscing about all the men they had known. How most had been losers, except, of course, for their dearly departed husbands. I hoped Madge and Helen didn't go back to Pete's to toast their old boyfriends. I wasn't up for a repeat of yesterday morning.

"'Mornin' ladies," I said in a cheery voice as I entered the salon. Madge and Helen were sitting on matching stools inside the front door. Trudy was already fussing over a client at her nail station.

"Did you notice it?" Madge asked.

"Notice what?"

"The salon's front window. Someone tried to break in last night. They put a big crack in it."

I hadn't noticed anything out of the ordinary, so I walked back outside to take a look. Sure enough, a tiny crack was running down the entire length of our large picture window. I wondered if it was the handiwork of the same guy who broke into my apartment last night. I was feeling a little paranoid as I stepped back inside.

"What do you think?" Helen asked, scratching one of her bare arms.

"The window needs to be replaced. What have you done about it?"

"I've already called my insurance agent," Madge replied. "He said to file a police report and obtain a few quotes on fixing the window before calling him back. I still can't figure out what he's supposed to do when a person has a claim."

Hmmm. Maybe I should have become an insurance agent. Sounds like they don't work all that hard.

I turned and walked back to my nail station. A half hour later, Mary Donovan strolled into the salon. What's she doing here? I hoped she hadn't broken a nail since Wednesday afternoon. I walked up front to greet her.

"What's going on, Mary?" I asked.

"I'm not here for my nails if you're wondering," she said. "Chief Cobb asked me to stop by and check out your front window. We're short-handed this morning. Most of the guys are helping the sheriff's department. A tractor-trailer overturned on County Road 40 and it's blocking everything in the area."

"You'd better talk to Madge," I said. "She'll tell you what she thinks happened."

Mary found Madge and Helen, who offered their theory on the cracked window. I went back to my nail station to get ready for my ten o'clock appointment. Twenty minutes later, Mary wandered back.

"Get everything you needed from Madge and Helen?" I asked.

"Yep," Mary said. "They're convinced it was an attempted break-in. I don't see how that's possible. It's a cracked window. Some festival entertainers were performing on the road in front of the nail salon last night. A few folks probably became too rambunctious and pushed a friend against the window. We hauled in more unruly rowdies than normal for a Thursday night."

"That's good to know, Mary. I thought it might be the same guy who broke into my place last night."

"Yeah, I heard about your break-in," Mary said. "I was on lunch break when Mandy called, but Nate and Frank told me later how you didn't find anything missing. Strange. Why would somebody break in and not take anything?"

"I talked to Dan at the diner this morning. He said it might have been the person responsible for Walter's murder."

"Interesting. I hear the Chief is having second thoughts about arresting Sylvia," Mary said. "He's been under a lot of pressure to solve the case. The town president wants the investigation wrapped up as soon as possible."

"Why's Dougie Drake so hot and bothered about Walter's murder?"

"He wants everything solved so people aren't afraid to come to town for the Foliage Festival. Your typical Chamber of Commerce-type paranoia."

"Right, like someone else will be murdered on the town square. This isn't Indianapolis or Chicago. It's Bartonsville. Murders don't happen here every day."

"You know how Dougie gets," Mary said. "This is also the Chief's first big case since becoming the head of the department. He's likely worried about making a good first impression with Dougie and members of the town council and getting the case solved quickly."

I nodded and walked Mary to the front door. She waved goodbye to Madge and Helen before leaving.

"I wish Chief Cobb had sent someone else."

"Why's that, Madge?"

"Mary Donovan doesn't know anything about police work. She's only a dispatcher. It's obvious to us it was an attempted break-in."

"Does it matter?" I said. "The guy didn't get in. Nothing was stolen."

My comment stopped Madge in her tracks. She began stammering and couldn't respond to my comment. Finally, Helen came to her rescue.

"Don't worry, Madge. I'll call Nate when he gets up in a little while. I'll have him drop by and look at the window. He'll know what to do."

"Whatever," I said throwing my arms in the air. I wandered back to my nail station to await my eleven o'clock appointment.

If Madge were this upset by a crack in her window, she would have really freaked if the burglar had broken in and left her a message on the mirror behind the front counter.

CHAPTER 23

When I finished with my client's nails, I told Madge and Helen that I needed to run a quick errand before my next client showed up. They were still sitting on their matching stools, chatting about why someone would want to break into the salon.

"Don't worry, Madge," I heard Helen say as I opened the front door. "Nate's on his way. He'll solve the mystery."

Brother.

My errand was to stop by Morrison's Office Supply, two doors down from the salon, to make a copy of Irene Morgan's death list. I planned to drop it in Johnny's lap and see if he could figure out its significance.

"That'll be a dollar," Betty Morrison said after returning from her Xerox machine with a copy of the list.

A dollar? Whew! At that price, I'm glad I wasn't copying a bunch of recipes.

I handed Betty the five-dollar tip that my last client had given me and received four crisp, dollar bills in return. Good. I just had enough money for lunch. Thank goodness, today's pay day. It will be nice to have some cash in my pocket again.

Next stop—the diner. It seemed extra busy today with some scruffy looking people I hadn't seen before. Must be the carnies in town for the festival enjoying a good home-cooked meal. Johnny was sitting at a table by himself.

"What's up, Candi?" he asked as I drew near.

"What are you eating?" I said, sitting down across from him. "I don't remember that on the menu."

"It's a vegetarian dish Ritchie makes especially for me," he said. "It's mostly vegetables, with some tofu tossed into the bowl. I need to watch what I eat because I'm chair bound."

"I've got another assignment for you," I said, pushing a sheet of paper across the table.

"What's this?"

"Irene Morgan gave it to me last night. She found it in one of Walter's suits. Notice how his name is crossed out. Irene thinks it's a death list."

"A death list? Do you?"

"Heck no, I think it's a list of the faux beauty contestants, but I don't know for sure. I'm hoping you can figure it out."

Johnny looked more closely at the list before he asked, "Who's Salty?"

"No idea. I thought you'd know."

"Nope. Must be somebody's nickname, but I've never heard of anyone called by that name."

"I'm hoping you can find out."

"I'll do my best."

Johnny left, but I continued sitting at the table and patted myself on the back for getting him to do my legwork. A moment later, Joanie brought me my lunch and sat down across from me.

"Sorry, I didn't get your lunch sooner," she said. "I wasn't expecting we'd be so busy today. It's like these carnival people haven't eaten in a week or more."

"Thanks, Joanie," I said, grabbing the sandwich and taking a big bite. "I wasn't in a hurry. I needed to share some information with Johnny."

"What was it?" she asked. "He literally threw his money at me as he left. Said something about having a new assignment to work on. I've never seen him move so fast."

I grinned and quickly filled Joanie in on the note Irene gave me and how I'd given a copy to Johnny to figure out what it meant.

"Think it's a death list?"

"No, of course not. But who knows? This way, at least, I won't get in trouble with Dan for sticking my nose in Walter's murder. He reminded me again this morning to stay out of his murder investigation. This way, Dan can get mad at Johnny if he's lucky enough to come up with anything."

"That's pretty devious, Candi."

I reached across the table and squeezed Joanie's hands. "Thanks."

"Can you do me a favor?" she asked.

"What's up?"

"My darling Patty called me a while ago. She came down with a migraine this morning and can't work the late shift. I'm doing a double, but if we're as busy at dinner time as we have been for lunch, I could use some help."

"Sure thing. I'll be here right after work."

Oh, boy, I'm back to slinging hash again.

CHAPTER 24

"Where's Madge?" I asked Trudy after returning to the nail salon a few minutes later.

"I'm not sure," she replied. "Madge left in a huff a minute ago."

"What's going on?"

"Like I said, I'm not sure," Trudy said, moving closer and lowering her voice. "I was finishing with a client and couldn't hear what Madge and Helen were saying. But, they definitely were having a spat."

"A spat, huh? That must be why Helen didn't say anything when I asked about Madge's whereabouts. She stared at me like I was a statute. What were they arguing about?"

"It had something to do about Helen wanting to put a handmade sign on the utility pole out front," Trudy said. "She wants festival goers to know she's selling her cosmetics and aromatherapy candles inside the salon. I don't think Madge liked the idea."

"I knew this would happen," I said, slapping the side of my leg. "You know how Madge is about the salon. She always wants us to act so professional in front of clients. It burns her up to think Helen wants everyone and his mother to come in off the street and buy her products."

"You're probably right, Candi. But, we can't worry about that now. There's Nate."

I spotted him giving his mother a big hug. He was here to investigate the crack in the front window. And, Madge would want to hear what he had to say.

"Trudy, get on your cell and find the number for Pete's Bar," I said. "I'm guessing Madge ended up there."

"What should I tell her if I get her on the phone?"

"Tell her Helen is threatening to light all her candles and burn down the nail salon. That should bring her back here soon enough."

Trudy looked at me like I'd lost my mind before she grinned and wandered off to use her phone. I walked up front to greet Nate.

"You here to investigate our attempted break-in?" I said.

"That's what I hear," he replied. "Where should I begin?"

"At the scene of the crime, of course. Let's go outside and take a look."

Nate and I stood on the sidewalk, staring at the cracked window for a few minutes. I was feeling a chill and asked Nate if we could step back inside. Once there, I made sure Helen was within earshot before I asked Nate what he thought happened to the front window.

"The front window definitely has a giant crack in it," he said.

"Think somebody was trying to break into the salon last night?"

"Heck, no," Nate replied. "If someone wanted to break in, they'd have tried jimmying the front door. It didn't look like anybody touched it."

I rest my case, your honor.

I glanced at Helen to see her reaction.

"Darling, are you sure it wasn't an attempted break in?" she asked.

"Absolutely, Mom. It looks like someone leaned or was pushed against the window."

"What's going on in here? Where's the fire department?"

Madge had just stormed through the front door.

"Welcome back, Madge," I said before filling her in on Nate's assessment of the cracked front window.

"Are you absolutely sure it's nothing more than a cracked window?" Madge asked Nate.

"Yes, ma'am," he replied.

"Okay, then. Thanks for stopping by," she said. "Now, everyone, back to work."

Nate looked at me. I shrugged and walked back to my nail station. Nate gave his mother a peck on the cheek and left.

A few minutes later, Lonnie Sparks came rushing through the front door.

"Candi, you've got to help me," she said, all out of breath.

"What's the matter, sweetie?"

"I broke one of my beautiful French nails this morning while opening a jar of marmalade. I've been in a panic ever since. I was hoping you weren't busy and could fix it before my Red Hat luncheon tomorrow."

"Not a problem," I said. "Have a seat."

I was about to apply a fake nail to Lonnie's finger when my cell phone rang.

"Who's playing the Star-Spangled Banner?" Lonnie asked.

"Oh, sorry, it's my ringtone," I said. "I'll be a sec."

I reached into my handbag and pulled out my pink phone. It was Martha Rae Folger.

"Want to make another manicure appointment?" I asked her.

"Not today, honey. I'm calling because I read in the *Beacon* this morning how you're raising money for Sylvia Wilson. I want to interview you on the radio."

"I guess it would be okay, but I'm busy right now. Lonnie Sparks is sitting in my chair. She has a nail emergency."

"Give her your phone."

I did as Martha Rae asked. A minute later, Lonnie handed me back my phone.

"Okay," Martha Rae said. "Everything's fine with Lonnie, so let's get ready to do the interview."

I looked across at Lonnie. She nodded her approval before reaching into her pocketbook and pulling out her iPad.

"Get ready, Candi, in three…two…and one."

"Welcome back, folks, to *Over the Back Fence*, our afternoon talk show where you can learn what your neighbors are saying about you behind your back," Martha Rae began. "This hour, I'm talking to Candi DeCarlo of the Tips & Toes Nail Salon on the south side of the town square. Candi is a terrific manicurist. She does my nails. But today we're talking about a very brave thing she's done this week. Are you still there, Candi?"

"I'm here, Martha Rae," I replied, clearing my throat. "Are we on the air?"

"Yup, sit back, relax and tell our listeners about the legal defense fund you've started for Sylvia Wilson."

I quickly put my hand over my cell and yelled for Madge to turn on WYMN. She was busy watching her soap operas on her portable TV. I then launched into my story on raising money for Sylvia. When I finished, Martha Rae asked, "So, why don't you think Sylvia murdered Walter Morgan?"

"Because she didn't see him on Monday night?"

"What are you saying, Candi?"

I told Martha Rae how Walter had asked Sylvia to meet him at the bank on Monday night, but canceled their appointment at the last minute.

"Surely the police have other evidence against Sylvia, or why would they lock her up?"

"They do, but it's bogus, too."

"What do you mean?"

I told her how the police found a bottle of nail polish in Sylvia's purse when they picked her up on Tuesday. It matched the color of Walter's painted nails. I also told her nail polish is the last thing Sylvia would carry in her purse because she's allergic to it.

"This sounds like an absolute travesty of justice," Martha Rae announced. "You've convinced me of Sylvia's innocence. Folks, stop whatever you're doing, and either write a check to the Sylvia Wilson legal defense fund or find one of Candi's donation jars around town and fill it full of cash."

"That's so cool, Martha Rae. Thanks for saying that."

"It's time we found out some real answers to poor Sylvia's plight. Folks, I'll be right back after this commercial."

It was another second or two before Martha Rae came back on the line.

"Thanks for explaining what's happened to Sylvia," Martha Rae said. "I had no idea what she was going through. We'll help her get out of this mess."

"I sure hope we can," I said and hung up the phone.

CHAPTER 25

had tossed my cell phone in my handbag and was getting ready to attend to Lonnie Sparks when Madge approached us.

"Candi, DeCarlo, what were you thinking?" she shouted.

"What are you talking about Madge?"

"Telling Martha Rae's listeners how Sylvia Wilson couldn't have murdered Walter Morgan," she said. "You're not a detective. You're a manicurist for Pete's sake."

"Why are you so upset? I was simply telling Martha Rae the truth."

"No, you made a laughingstock of yourself and Tips & Toes. Who's going to believe that fantastic story of yours?" Madge said. "Nobody, that's who. This is so embarrassing. It'll likely ruin my business. I have half a notion to fire you right now."

"No, you won't," Lonnie Sparks interjected. "Now, Madge, calm down and listen to me. Candi didn't do anything wrong.

She was speaking from her heart. I happen to believe she's right. Sylvia had no reason to murder Walter Morgan. There are lots of other people who had more of a motive to kill him. So, back off on blaming Candi. Go back up front and watch your silly soap operas. Besides, you can't fire Candi. She hasn't finished fixing my broken French nail."

"Well…I never…in my entire life," Madge said, as she marched back to the front of the salon.

"Thanks, Lonnie," I said once Madge was out of earshot.

"No problem," she replied. "If she fires you, let me know. I'll call all of your clients and we'll boycott this place. Now, get busy and fix my nail. I have a four o'clock tanning bed appointment at Sun & Suds. I don't want to be late. I need to look perfect for my Red Hat tea tomorrow."

"Yes ma'am." I quickly went to work on Lonnie's broken nail and had her out of the salon well before her tanning appointment. She was so thankful that she left me a bigger tip than normal and twenty bucks for Sylvia's defense fund. No sooner had Lonnie left, then several women entered the salon. And, it wasn't to check out Helen's aromatherapy candles.

"Where's this Candi DeCarlo person I heard on Martha Rae's show?" asked one woman who I'd never seen before. "I want to write her a check for fifty dollars. While I'm at it, let me make an appointment for a manicure next week. I haven't had my nails done in a long time."

A tiny smile flashed across Madge's face as she wrote the woman's name in our appointment book.

"Think Madge will fire you?" Trudy asked when I walked back to my nail station.

"I hope not, but who knows. She seemed pretty mad at me."

"She's not mad at you," Trudy explained. "It's Helen."

"Huh?"

"Yeah, Madge realizes she made a mistake by letting Helen move into the salon with her cosmetics and aromatherapy candles. Madge doesn't like people traipsing into the salon and pawing through Helen's merchandise. Didn't you see how crowded it was earlier?"

"Not really. I was too busy talking to Martha Rae and fixing Lonnie's nail. But, we'll know soon enough. We only have another hour before closing time."

"Stop worrying about getting fired," Trudy said, gently patting me on my shoulder. "Trust me, Madge has bigger fish to fry."

Bigger fish to fry? I was surprised by Trudy's bold statement. She's usually so timid about saying anything bad. Did she know something I didn't? I had noticed this morning that Madge and Helen didn't seem as cheery as they did on their visit to Pete's Bar the other day. And, why was Trudy suddenly so concerned about me? It's weird. Maybe, she's human after all.

I checked the appointment book. I didn't have another client this afternoon. That suited me just fine. I could clean up my nail station early and leave for the diner as soon as Madge paid us and closed the salon for the night.

My cell phone rang as I finished wiping down my station. It was Mandy.

"I hear you stirred up a hornet's nest earlier today."

"What are you talking about?" I asked.

"I talked to Nate."

"Not again?"

"It's okay. He only gave me a warning this time. Said if he gave me another speeding ticket, the prosecutor might file charges against me for having two speeding tickets in a single week."

"Bless his heart. What did you do?" I asked.

"I gave him a peck on his cheek."

"How did he react?"

"His face became red. I could have sworn hearing him say, 'aw shucks.'"

"Okay, that explains your hornet's nest. What did Nate say about mine?"

He mentioned hearing you on Martha Rae's talk show this afternoon and how you spilled the beans on why Sylvia Wilson didn't murder Walter Morgan. Nate said Chief Cobb is livid with you and your big mouth."

"Oops," I said. "But Mandy, you know me. I was only being truthful with Martha Rae."

"I know, honey, but you need to remember the big shots in town don't like controversy. They hate it when someone comes along and disrupts the proverbial apple cart. Sounds like whatever you told Martha Rae has turned the murder investigation upside down. Instead of apples, the bigwigs now have applesauce on their faces."

"That's a pretty interesting image there, Mandy," I said. "But I don't care. Sylvia's innocent, and that's all that matters to me."

"Want to have dinner tonight?" Mandy asked.

"I can't. Patty's sick and can't work tonight so I'm helping Joanie. But, I'm free tomorrow night."

Before we hung up, Mandy and I agreed to get together after work on Saturday. We would check out the vendor's booths at the annual Foliage Festival and eat at Ralph's.

As I put my phone away, I looked up and saw Madge motion for me and Trudy to join her at the front counter. I checked my watch. We still had a half hour before closing time.

"Here's your checks, girls," she said, handing us our weekly pay. "Don't spend it all at the festival tonight. I've checked our appointment book. We have a busy day tomorrow. Go home early and get some rest."

Trudy spoke up. "Does this mean you're not firing Candi?"

Madge looked at her with a surprised look on her face.

"No, Trudy, I'm not firing Candi. What gave you that idea? Yes, I was upset with her earlier for what she said on Martha Rae's radio show. However, I now see how folks in town share her feelings about Sylvia's innocence. So, let's forget that ever happened, okay?"

Trudy gave me a big wink before grabbing her hoodie from the coatrack and leaving. I was stunned but couldn't figure out if it was because of Trudy's wink or Madge's feeble attempt at apologizing.

"Candi, drop off the night deposit," Madge said. "Helen and I have things to talk about."

"Whatever you say, Madge."

"You also need to deposit the money in your donation jar," Madge added. "I counted it earlier. There's nearly two hundred dollars in bills and checks. I don't want to leave it here tonight in case the burglar shows up again."

I grabbed the money from Madge's hand and wandered back to my nail station to pick up my handbag. I also looked at my watch. Twenty to six. If I hurried, I could make it to the bank in time to open a bank account for Sylvia's fund.

The town square was filled with people enjoying the brightly colored carnival rides set up on the streets surrounding the square and the vendor booths on the courthouse lawn. However, the bank was virtually empty as I made my way to Louise Dorfman's teller's window.

"Here's our night deposit," I said, handing Louise the salon's money bag. "I also want to open an account for Sylvia Wilson's legal defense fund."

"I heard you were a hit on Martha Rae's show today," Louise said, giving me a giant smile. "Several people wanted to give us some money for Sylvia. I had to tell them you hadn't opened a bank account yet. They'd have to come back another day."

"So, let's get one opened."

"I wish I could help you, but only Jane Parker can open an account like that."

"Is Miz Parker still here?"

"No, she had an important meeting with the town president and left early. I don't expect her back before we close."

I looked at my watch. It was now ten minutes to six.

"Got to go. I'm working at Ralph's tonight."

CHAPTER 26

"There she is," someone yelled as I walked into the diner a few minutes later.

"You go, girl," a female voice shouted while several others stood up from their all-you-can-eat catfish dinners and began clapping. What a welcome. It felt as if I'd been crowned the Foliage Festival Queen.

"What's going on?" I asked Joanie. She was busy making change at the cash register for a farmer dressed in neatly pressed overalls.

"Duh?" Joanie said. "They heard you on Martha Rae's show. You're Bartonsville's newest local hero. Defender of the innocent and downtrodden. There's more money in your donation jar than in the cash register."

I smiled. "They believed me."

"Go figure, but now isn't the time for idle chitchat," Joanie said. "I've been swamped for the past hour. Hang up that animal on your back, grab an apron, and lend me a hand."

Business continued non-stop during my first hour at the diner. So much for people worrying about visiting the town square after Walter Morgan's murder. These folks didn't have a care in the world other than seeing how quickly they could stuff themselves with Ritchie's lightly breaded, deep-fried catfish. I'm told it's the best around, but I've never tasted it. I'm not into fish. Give me red meat, cooked medium-well, anytime.

"Do me a favor, Candi, and deliver these two plates to table eight," Joanie said as we stood in front of the pass-through window. "I need to clear some tables, so I can seat the people lined up at the door."

I grabbed the plates, but before delivering them, I took off my five-inch stilettos and left them behind the lunch counter. They were killing my feet and slowing me down. As I approached table eight, I realized I was delivering dinner to Dougie Drake and Jane Parker.

"Back to being a waitress again, Candi?"

Dougie's such a jerk. I wanted to toss his dinner on his head. But, I knew Ritchie and Joanie wouldn't approve. So, I placed his tenderloin dinner on the table in front of him. Jane was having a diet fruit plate.

"No, Mister Town President, I'm simply helping Joanie out tonight. She's shorthanded."

Jane Parker must have sensed that I was upset with Dougie's smart aleck remark. She changed the subject.

"Louise called me after locking up the bank and said you dropped by to open an account for Sylvia Wilson," Jane said. "I'm sorry I wasn't there. I had to make a quick trip out of town. However, if you can drop by before we close at noon tomorrow, I'll open an account for you."

"Thanks, Jane," I said.

"Why open a defense fund for Sylvia Wilson now that you've blabbed to everyone in town that you think she's innocent?" Dougie asked.

"You heard me on the radio?"

"No, but lots of others listen to that damn gossipy show," Dougie said, with a disgusted look on his face. "Everybody knows Martha Rae Folger is a busybody. She's had a vendetta against me for years. Thinks she knows how to run this town better than me. Those who called me after her show demanded that I talk to the police chief and prosecutor and have Sylvia Wilson released immediately."

"Did you talk to them?"

"No," Dougie said, pounding his fist on the table. "Why would I do that? I told you the other day. Sylvia's guilty of murdering Walter. But, no, you had to keep nosing around and riling everyone up. If anything, I should have the prosecutor charge you with obstructing justice. And, who knows? Maybe you conspired with Sylvia to murder Walter. After all, the cops found you in his office."

"Go ahead, but the prosecutor won't get anywhere," I said, staring back at Dougie. "The truth is on my side."

"We'll see about that," Dougie said before taking a bite of his tenderloin.

I turned and stomped back to the pass-through window.

"What was going on over there?" Joanie asked. "Dougie seemed upset. Was his tenderloin not big enough to suit him? All the folks sitting nearby stopped eating and were eavesdropping on your conversation."

"Dougie still believes Sylvia murdered Walter."

"What?" Joanie replied. "Does he live in a dream world? Must be the same one every other politician lives in. Everyone in town knows Sylvia didn't do it, thanks to you."

"That's right," I said. "And thanks for the compliment."

"Don't mention it."

As we turned around from the pass-through window, Joanie spotted Dougie waving at us.

"What does he want now?" I asked.

"Don't worry. Let me handle him," Joanie said, walking toward Dougie's table.

The dinner crowd didn't let up until nearly eight o'clock. I've never seen so many people eat so much catfish at one time, in one place. I don't get it. Catfish is so icky looking, but I'm told it tastes good. Poor Ritchie. I wonder if he makes any money with his all-you-can-eat specials.

"So, what did Dougie want?" I asked Joanie when she came back to the lunch counter.

"A refill of his sweet tea."

"That was it?"

"No, he also complained about you. Said I should fire you on the spot for not wearing any shoes. Said it was probably a health department violation, and he intended to check into it."

"Did you tell him I was helping out tonight, and my feet didn't touch any of the food?"

"Yeah, but it didn't make him any less angry with you," Joanie said. "The guy's a jerk. Don't worry about him. He gulped down his sweet tea and left with Jane."

As we continued talking, someone sitting near the front entrance suddenly shrieked. Joanie and I both looked up to see what was going on.

Sylvia Wilson just walked through the front door.

CHAPTER 27

It was nearly ten-thirty before I made it home. I was exhausted and could barely keep my eyes open. It had been an awfully long day. A real roller coaster of a day, but even with my eyelids half shut, I was so excited by what happened when Sylvia walked into the diner.

Ritchie quickly locked the front door, telling one couple approaching the diner that the place was now closed for a private party. He then asked Sylvia if there was anything he could do for her.

"Sure is," she said with a slight grin. "It probably won't be good for my digestive tract and I may live to regret it, but I'd love one of your big juicy cheeseburgers and some fries. I hated the grub they served at the jail."

As we waited on Ritchie to finish preparing Sylvia's burger, she told me and Joanie how Chief Cobb ordered her release after going over her story again on where she'd been on Monday and Tuesday.

"I still don't know why it took him so long to change his mind," I said when Sylvia finished.

"If I had to guess, I'd say he was still troubled over the pink nail polish bottle in my purse," Sylvia said. "It definitely made it look like I had something to do with Walter's murder."

"I can understand that," I said, "but, you didn't meet Walter on Monday night. Did you tell him how Walter called and canceled your meeting?"

"Yes, and I even let him look at the text messages on my cell phone."

"Did he say anything about the incriminating evidence he found on Walter's desk?"

"Not really," Sylvia said. "I got the impression that he had a change of heart about my involvement with whatever was in that folder."

"Interesting."

Ritchie brought out the biggest cheeseburger I'd ever seen him make. He placed it in front of Sylvia with an extra-large order of fries. The rest of us then sat there and watched Sylvia devour the whole thing. Twenty minutes later, nothing was left on the plate. Sylvia let out a sigh and wiped her chin. It was a job well done.

"Now I'm ready to go home," she announced.

"Your carriage awaits you out back," I said, escorting Sylvia to my truck. When we arrived at her house, I gave her a big hug and promised to call her on Saturday to see how she was doing.

Once at my place, I found myself unable to fall asleep right away even though I was dead tired. I sat in my rocking chair, still mulling my conversation with Sylvia. I needed to talk to someone about it. I thought about calling Sylvia, but she seemed so tired and frail from her ordeal in jail. She probably was already sound asleep. Mandy was my next choice.

I jumped up from my rocker, grabbed my landline phone, and dialed her number.

"What are you doing?" I asked when she picked up.

"Sleeping."

"I'm sorry, but I need to talk."

"Okay," she replied, "Talk away while I try to wake up."

I told Mandy how Sylvia was sprung from jail, but I was still wondering how the nail polish bottle ended up in her purse.

"Does Sylvia have any clues?"

"No, on Monday and Tuesday, she was too busy handing out posters for the Youth Center's fundraiser tomorrow night to notice if anyone slipped the bottle in her purse. Johnny tried retracing her steps, using the list she gave me, but he couldn't figure out where the nail polish came from either."

Then, it hit me. If Dan let Sylvia go, it was for one of two reasons. Either he decided the nail polish bottle was no longer crucial to his investigation, or he had figured out who owned it. I described my theory to Mandy.

"That's probably it," Mandy said. "Congratulations, Sherlock."

"Thanks, so maybe I should talk to Dan, and see if he'll tell me who his new suspect is."

"Fine. Go for it. Now, can I go back to sleep?"

How can you sleep at a time like this?

CHAPTER 28

On Saturday morning as I started my truck's ignition, I spotted a piece of paper stuck under the wiper blade. Oops. It better not be another parking ticket. I still hadn't paid the ones in my glove compartment. And, here I thought it was okay to park on Elm Street at night.

I climbed out of the truck, grabbed the paper, and jumped back in before another blast of cold Arctic air hit me in the face. Winter was on its way, but I was ready, thanks to my warm rabbit fur jacket.

I glanced at the paper and realized it wasn't a parking ticket after all. That was a relief, but what was it?

"Mind your own business, or else!" the note read. Somebody had used a red crayon to write it, but it didn't look like the work of one of the neighborhood's juvenile delinquents. The words were all spelled correctly. It also had that mark at the end of the sentence. What's it called again? Oh, yeah, I remember. An exclamation mark. No, this message was the work of a delinquent adult.

I crumbled the paper and tossed it on my passenger seat. Someone's trying to scare me. Well, I've got news for him. It's not working. After letting my truck warm up for another minute, I took off. At the stop sign a block away, I flipped on WYMN. It was just seven-thirty. Time for the morning news.

"Finally, this breaking news story," Caroline Tinsdale, the station's news and farm director, said. "We've learned the police released Sylvia Wilson last night. She's no longer a suspect in Walter Morgan's murder. That's great news. Keep listening to WYMN throughout the day as we learn if the police have another suspect in mind. Now for the weather...."

I shut off the radio and wondered if McPherson had written a similar story for this morning's *Beacon*. I was anxious to get to the diner to find out. Five minutes later, I parked in the lot behind Tips & Toes and walked around the corner.

Ahead of me, two scruffy looking teens were sauntering down the sidewalk. When they reached the front of the nail salon, they stopped and pointed at the window. As I drew closer, I could see why the teens had stopped dead in their tracks.

On the plywood covering the cracked window was a handmade sign written in big red letters. "Mind your own business, or else!"

Oh no, this had all the makings of a bad day. I grabbed the front door and stepped inside.

"Did you see that sign out front?" Madge bellowed before I had time to close the door. "Got any idea where it might have come from?"

"Nope."

"Well, I bet I know," she said in a razor-sharp voice.

The jig was up. Madge must have heard the WYMN newscast, too.

"Candi, I'm glad to hear Sylvia was released from jail, but I'm scared for you," she said. "The sign outside isn't the work of some festivalgoer. It was intended for you and it has to do with Walter's murder. It's why I called the police. They're on their way here."

"Thanks, Madge," I said, making my way to my nail station where Trudy accosted me.

"Notice the sign on the front window?" she asked. "What's it mean?"

I looked Trudy straight in the eye. "It means somebody's threatening me for sticking my nose in business that doesn't concern me. But, I don't want to talk about it, okay?"

"Sure, Candi, whatever you say," Trudy said with a surprised look on her face. "I hope it all works out for you."

"I do, too," I replied and began preparing my nail station for today's clients.

Five minutes later, Dan walked into the nail salon.

"Wow," I heard Madge tell him. "When I called the station a few minutes ago, I wasn't expecting them to send you, Chief. But I'm glad you're here."

"I need to speak to Candi," he said as he continued walking in my direction. He stopped in front of me. "We need to talk."

I didn't like the expression on Dan's face. He wasn't smiling like he usually does when he greets me. I was in for a tongue lashing. Better make it in private, out of earshot of Madge and Trudy. I motioned for Dan to follow me into the storage room. Once I closed the door, he started in on me.

"Where should I begin?" Dan said, crossing his arms and staring intently at me.

"While you're deciding, can I tell you how much I appreciate you setting Sylvia free last night? It was a big relief to her and those of us who always believed in her innocence."

"This is all a big joke to you, isn't it?"

"What do you mean?"

"You gloss over everything that's happened this week by making a smart aleck comment."

"I was not being that way just now. I am honestly thankful for what you did for Sylvia."

"Okay," Dan said as he sat down in one of the folding chairs we keep in the storage room. I followed his lead and jumped up on the storage room folding table. I might as well get comfortable. This had all the makings of a long conversation.

"I accept your thanks," Dan said, "but you need to realize the people who murdered Walter Morgan are still out there and they don't want to be found. If you're wondering who wrote that message on the salon's front window this morning, it probably was the killers."

"I know," I said, lowering my head. "The same message was left on my truck's windshield this morning."

"See what I'm talking about?" Dan said, pointing his finger at me. "These people don't want you nosing around in Walter's murder. I can only imagine how angry they were when they heard you on the radio yesterday."

"Did you hear me on the radio?"

"No, but I heard from everyone else who listened. It included the town president all the way to the guy who cleans the police station at night. Everyone had an opinion. Douglas Drake still thinks Sylvia killed Walter Morgan, but the majority of the others I talked to thought Sylvia was innocent, and I should release her."

"Is that why you let her go?"

"No, it had more to do with what she told me during my interview with her. Sylvia Wilson is allergic to nail polish and had no reason to carry that bottle around in her purse."

"How come you believed her yesterday, and not when you first talked to her?"

"She didn't provide me with a good answer during her initial interview. She acted like she was hiding something. But after talking to you, I realized Sylvia likely was frightened at being taken into custody and wasn't thinking straight when we first spoke. After all, she doesn't have a police record. Not even a parking ticket."

Sylvia's got one on me.

"I'm glad I could help solve that mystery. You don't have to thank me again if you don't want to. Once is enough."

"Huh?"

There I go being a smart aleck again.

I quickly changed the subject. "What about the incriminating evidence you found on Walter's desk? You felt it had to do with Sylvia."

"We came to the conclusion it didn't directly implicate her, but I can't say anything more about it."

"So, do you have any new suspects?" I asked.

"Officially not yet, but I have a couple of people in mind," Dan said. "It's why I need to ask you a few more questions. Tell me again what time you went to the bank looking for Walter Morgan on Monday night?"

"It was well after six o'clock, but I don't remember exactly."

"Candi, try to focus on that day again. It's important for you to come up with an exact time. It may hold the key to solving this case."

I didn't appreciate the sudden pressure Dan was putting on me. Wanting me to remember the exact time I showed up at Walter's office. But I had to try. Let's see. Walter normally showed up for his nail appointments at six. It seemed like an eternity when he didn't arrive on Monday night. I remembered looking down at my Betty Boop watch at least once. It read 6:45 p.m.

"Are you absolutely sure?" Dan asked when I told him.

"Positive."

"Wait a minute," I said remembering something Sylvia told me last night. "Sylvia said you looked at her cell phone to see when Walter canceled his appointment with her. I called Walter twice on Monday night when he didn't show up for his appointment. I have this thing about people being punctual. Anyway, you're welcome to look at my phone."

"Absolutely," Dan said sitting up straight in the folding chair.

I ran to my nail station, grabbed my cell phone and rushed back to the storage room.

"Here you go," I said, handing Dan my phone.

He looked at it closely for a few minutes before writing down some information in the notebook he'd taken out of his suit jacket. He then stood up, closed his notebook, handed back my phone, and left the storage room without even saying goodbye.

"Glad I could help, Dan" I said to myself as I walked out of the storage room. A minute later. Madge was all over me like melting butter on toast.

"What were you doing in there with Chief Cobb?" she asked. "You were in there forever."

"It's not what you're thinking. Dan had some more questions about my visit to Walter Morgan's office on Monday night."

"Why? I thought you only went there to talk to him about buying a salon gift certificate for his wife's birthday."

"It's true," I said, crossing the fingers on both hands behind my back. "But Dan needed to know the exact time. Since he no longer suspects me or Sylvia of killing Walter, he's trying to nail down the exact time when the true killers murdered him."

"Oh…so, did he say anything about the message left out front?"

"Yeah, he said it was probably the work of Walter's killers. Sending me a message to butt out."

"Omigod," Madge exclaimed as she clutched her chest. "You're going to give me a heart attack."

"Do I need to call the paramedics?"

"No, I can't worry about it now," she said. "Clients are backing up on us. Go to your nail station, and I'll send one back to you."

As I stood by my station waiting on my first client of the day, Trudy sidled up to me and muttered in a low voice. "Notice anything unusual this morning?"

"Are you talking about the message left out front?"

"No, I assume that's what you and Chief Cobb talked about in the storage room. I'll give you a hint," Trudy said. "Look up front and tell me what you see."

"Helen's gone."

I hadn't noticed she was missing when I first walked into the salon this morning. I was still in a daze. I hadn't yet had a Diet Dr. Pepper to help me wake up.

"Yes. All her smelly old candles, too."

"Did Madge tell you why Helen isn't here?" I asked.

"No, I was afraid to ask. I wasn't sure what her reaction would be."

Fraidy cat.

I wanted to call Trudy out for not finding what happened with Helen, but I didn't get the chance. Some high school girl plopped down in my chair and said, "I want a set of fakes that look like these." She showed me a gossip magazine photo of Taylor Swift waving to her adoring fans.

It was nearly twelve thirty before I had a chance to catch my breath. Besides the high school girl, I had another client who wanted a pair of acrylics and one with a broken nail.

"Do I have time to run to the diner and grab a carryout order?" I asked Madge. "I didn't have any breakfast this morning. I'm starving."

"Go ahead, but don't take all day. Madeline Owens will be here at one-fifteen and you know how she is if she has to wait."

Madeline has the punctual gene in triplicate.

"I'll be right back."

I ran down the street as fast as I could in my five-inch stilettos. I was dying to see if McPherson was there. I wondered if he'd written a story about Sylvia's release from jail.

I stepped inside the diner and immediately looked for him munching on his usual cheeseburger deluxe in the back booth. He wasn't there. A pair of carnies were sitting there instead. I grabbed an empty stool at the lunch counter and waited for Joanie. She was busy delivering some food to her other customers.

"Seen McPherson?" I asked when she came back to the counter.

"Nope, he hasn't shown up for lunch yet."

"That's odd. He's always here by this time, even on Saturdays."

"I know, and it's not like him to miss a meal," Joanie said. "Maybe he's busy working on another exclusive."

"I call that dedication. Can I have my usual to-go today? I need to get back to the salon. We were swamped this morning."

"Sure thing. I'm sorry I can't come along and give you a hand like you helped me last night. I don't do nails."

After Joanie left to retrieve my lunch, I leaned into the guy sitting next to me and asked if I could read the front page of his newspaper. He was busy looking at the sports section.

McPherson had a front-page story about Sylvia's release, but nothing more than what WYMN reported this morning. Too bad he hadn't stopped by the diner for a late dinner last night. He could have had an exclusive. Maybe, that's where he is now. Rapping on poor Sylvia's door and demanding that she wake up and talk to him. Pushy news people.

A minute later Joanie put my lunch in front of me. I stood up and reached in my handbag for money to pay her.

"By the way, I forgot to mention it before. I noticed a piece of paper on the window of your truck as I walked past your place on my way to work this morning. Another parking ticket?"

"No, it was a message from Walter's murderers."

CHAPTER 29

made it back to Tips & Toes just after one o'clock. Madeline Owens hadn't shown up yet. But Anne Taylor had. She and her TV crew were sitting patiently in our reception area.

"Hello, Miz Castle, or is it Candi DeCarlo?" Anne asked. "Your boss told me your real name."

"Yeah, sorry about that the other day," I said. "It must have been this new medication my doctor prescribed for me. It makes me forgetful sometimes. So, what can I do for you today, Miz Taylor?"

"We've heard the police released Sylvia Wilson last night as the prime suspect in Walter Morgan's murder. We want your reaction to that news and what you plan to do with the money that you collected for her legal defense."

"Okay," I said. "Want to do the interview outside again?"

"No," Anne said. "There's too much noise out there with those festival rides. Can we do it inside the nail salon instead?"

"Make sure you finish your interview before Madeline shows up," Madge said.

"Who's Madeline?" Anne asked as we walked back to my nail station.

"She's one of my clients," I replied. "Madeline believes she deserves special treatment. She can wait, or Madge can take care of her. Besides, Madeline doesn't tip that well. Let's do the interview."

It took Anne's cameraman a few minutes to set his camera on a tripod in front of my nail station. While he did that, Anne took out a compact from a pocket in her trench coat and checked her makeup.

"I'm ready," she said a few minutes later after taking off her coat. She sat down at my station and thrust her microphone in my face.

"Wow," I said. "Your nails are lovely. Where do you have them done?"

"I go to a little shop near our TV station," Anne replied. "The little Asian woman there does nice work."

"I'll say, but I would love the opportunity to do your nails sometime," I said. "I've never done the nails of a celebrity like yourself."

I swear Anne blushed at my comment, but she quickly brought the conversation back to Sylvia. We spent the next ten minutes talking about her being set free and how I thought the money for her legal defense fund would now go towards the renovations at the Youth Center. When Anne ran out of questions, I asked her one.

"Did you talk to Chief Cobb? Did he say anything about who he now suspects for Walter's murder?"

"No, he didn't tell us anything," Anne said. "In fact, he refused to meet with us."

"I'm surprised," I said. "He's always been willing to talk with me."

"But you don't shove a mic in his face. Frankly, I wasn't surprised by his reaction. He's kind of boring."

"Is that why you only went out once with him?"

"How'd you know that?"

"You told me the other night."

"I did, didn't I. Yeah, he's a nice enough guy, but not too adventuresome. Not a problem. I ended up dating a tight end with the Indianapolis Colts."

Some women have all the luck.

Soon after Anne and her TV crew left the salon, Madeline Owens showed up.

"So sorry, I'm late, Candi," she said. "I ran into an old friend at the festival and completely lost track of time."

"Not a problem, Madeline," I said. "I was busy doing a TV interview."

"What? A TV interview. Why would someone interview you?"

"It was Action News," I said. "They asked me about Sylvia Wilson and the money I raised for her legal defense."

"Oh," Madeline said. "I heard something about that on Martha Rae's radio show. It was genuinely nice of you, Candi."

"Thanks," I replied. "Now, what would you like me to do with your nails?"

"Same old thing is okay."

It took me a little over forty minutes to give Madeline a new set of French nails and send her on her way. And, yes, she only gave me a five-dollar tip.

"Did that woman get your name right this time?"

"What are you talking about, Trudy?"

"One of my clients told me about you being on TV the other night. Said they called you Trudy Castle. Is that right?"

"Afraid so," I replied. "It was unfortunate, but it goes to show that you can't trust the news media. They're always getting stuff wrong. It's why I wrote my name down on one of the salon's business cards today."

"That was a good idea, Candi," Trudy said. "I've got another question. Did you run into McPherson at the diner?"

"No," I replied. "Why are you asking?"

"I dunno. Madge was talking about him after you left to pick up your lunch. Said he was interviewed on the WYMN newscast at noon. He was talking about how Sylvia didn't murder Walter Morgan."

Wow. I couldn't believe Trudy. She generally isn't interested in talking about anything other than how wonderful her husband, Keith, is or how she found a new technique in *Nails* Magazine for applying acrylic nails. Wonders never cease.

The rest of the afternoon wasn't much different from the morning. I couldn't believe how many regulars were getting all gussied up for the Foliage Festival, but then again, it's the town's only social event between now and the first Monday in December. That's when the town workers light the large pine tree in front of the courthouse. The lighting ceremony officially marks the beginning of Bartonsville's holiday season.

"You girls worked hard today," Madge said as she wandered back to our nail stations before five o'clock. "Our clients seemed happy with your efforts, so I'm letting you go home early."

Wow. That's awfully big of you, Madge, considering our appointment book doesn't show any more clients today.

I wanted to say that, but I didn't. No sense upsetting Madge when she's in a generous mood. Let's face it. It doesn't happen all that often.

"Going to check out the festival vendors?" I asked Madge as she finished preparing the bank deposit at the front counter.

"Heavens, no," she replied. "Who'd be dumb enough to buy that craft stuff sold on the courthouse lawn? I'm headed to the riverboat with my girlfriends."

I thought Madge was being a little harsh about the vendors. I've picked up some nice bargains over the years. However, I suppose if you own a nail salon, you can afford more expensive tastes.

"I didn't see Helen today," I said. "Is everything okay between the two of you?"

"Candi, I know what you're trying to do," Madge said. "You want to know what happened between us last night. Why can't you be more like Trudy and not ask me anything?"

"We both know Trudy only thinks of herself and her husband," I said. "I, on the other hand, am always looking out for everyone's emotional wellbeing. Especially yours, Madge."

I was ashamed of myself for being so over the top with my comment, but sometimes you have to do whatever it takes to get a person talking to you. I hoped it worked on Madge.

"Let's just say Helen and I had a difference of opinion on how I should run my business," Madge said. "Paying me a paltry sum of money for rent didn't give her the right to tell me what to do."

Okay. Madge finally stood up to Helen. You go, girl.

"Now, Candi, I need to get the night deposit ready and leave for the riverboat. If you keep asking me all these silly questions, I'll make you handle the deposit."

Once Madge finished putting the night deposit together. I grabbed it from her, as well as my jacket and handbag, and headed for the front door.

"Madge, I'm sticking around for the festival, so I'll take the night deposit to the bank for you."

"Thanks, Candi."

I had strolled halfway around the town square, admiring the new vendor booths, when I ran into Nate. He was stuffing his face with a greasy Philly cheese steak sandwich.

"How is it?" I asked.

"Yummy," I thought I heard him say as he tried swallowing what was still in his mouth.

"Had any problems?"

"Nope," he said. "Everyone is in a good mood and on their best behavior. I wish I didn't have to work overtime. I'd like to check out the new carnival rides."

Nate has always loved carnival rides. In high school, he'd spend every night at the festival riding the Tilt-a-Whirl, getting off only to take a bathroom break or grab something to eat.

"Seen Johnny Edwards today?" I asked.

"No, now that you mention it. I haven't seen him. That's strange. He's usually wheeling around here like a mad man getting into everyone's business."

"If you run into him, tell him I'm looking for him," I said. I was curious to learn if he'd had any luck tracking down the names on Irene Morgan's death list.

"What about McPherson?"

"Yeah, I saw him a minute ago with his camera," Nate said. "He was taking a picture of a little blonde-haired girl eating some cotton candy. She had it all over her face."

Like you're not wearing part of your Philly steak sandwich on yours.

"Sounds like a cute photo. I'm glad he's still on the job. I was afraid he might have been fired after leaking his story about Sylvia's release to WYMN this morning."

"I didn't hear it myself," Nate said. "I arrived home after working all night and went straight to bed. But I did run into Dougie Drake an hour ago. He told me all about it. He wasn't a happy camper."

"What do you mean?"

"Dougie said he couldn't believe McPherson was talking about Sylvia being innocent."

"Sounds like the same conversation I had with Dougie last night at the diner. He can't seem to let it go. What's his beef with Sylvia anyway?"

"Who knows," Nate said. "Just promise me you won't hit him with your handbag if you run into him tonight. You know how he is. He's likely to file assault charges against you. Remember what he was like in high school? Every time one of the jocks pushed him against the lockers, he ran off to the principal's office."

"You're right, Nate. Dougie is a wus."

Nate let out a huge belly laugh and slapped me on the back before walking away. He headed for the food truck, no doubt looking for a candy apple. I, on the other hand, checked my watch. It was 5:30 p.m. I'd better get busy if I intended to find a Christmas gift for my daughter.

CHAPTER 30

Ten minutes later, I realized that I forgot to ask Nate about his mother and Madge parting ways.

Candi, you're losing it.

Oh, well, I'd run into him later. All I needed to do was look for him at one of the festival's food trucks.

It took me only five minutes to find the perfect Christmas gift for my daughter.

It was at Woody the Woodman's booth. Woody, a tall, grandfatherly looking man wearing a blue Indianapolis Colts baseball cap, told me he could create Jenny's name from a block of wood in less than fifteen minutes. And, it'd cost me only twenty dollars. I figured Jenny might like a nameplate now that she was starting her new job as a paralegal at a large law firm in Indianapolis. A wooden one would look much nicer than those standard metal ones you see on people's desks.

While I watched Woody make Jenny's nameplate on his carving machine, I called Mandy to see if we were still on for having dinner. I hadn't heard from her all day. Mandy's home phone rang four times before her answering machine kicked on. I left her a message and hung up.

Woody wasn't finished yet, so I wandered off in search of other bargains. Maybe I could finish the rest of my Christmas shopping tonight.

It was nearing six and getting dark when I doubled back to Woody's booth to pick up Jenny's nameplate. Woody had done a beautiful job. It looked great. Jenny was going to love it.

With my gifts for Madge and Trudy—I bought them matching glass Christmas ornaments—clutched in my hand, I headed to my truck, which was parked behind Tips & Toes.

My plan was to leave the gifts there before walking back to Ralph's to meet Mandy for dinner. All that shopping had made me hungry.

I carefully placed my purchases behind my truck's front seat before closing and locking the doors. As I turned around, two guys dressed in matching dark blue sweatsuits and black ski masks pulled over their faces were staring at me. The shorter one of the two was pointing a gun at me. I suddenly had a flashback to my confrontation with Nate and Frank inside Walter's bank on Monday night.

"What's going on?" I asked, trying to remain calm. But I was scared out of my wits. I had no idea what these two had in mind. Judging by their expensive-looking sweatsuits, I figured they weren't interested in stealing my Christmas gifts.

"Don't scream, Miz DeCarlo," the taller one said. "We have no intention of harming you. We simply need you to come with us."

"Where?" I asked, relieved that I wasn't about to be robbed. Who were these people? And how did they know my name?

"Don't worry, it's a safe place," the taller one assured me. "Now, if you'll please turn around."

I stood still as the taller one carefully placed a hood over my head and pulled it snug, using a golden-colored string at the bottom of the hood.

"Can you breathe, Miz DeCarlo?" he asked.

No, I'm suffocating. Take it off.

I wanted to say that, but I didn't. These guys weren't likely to change their minds. If anything, the shorter one seemed more inclined to shoot me and be done with it.

"Let's get going," he said. I wasn't sure what would happen next. It's not every day I walk around with a hood over my head so I couldn't see.

"Stop," the shorter one said abruptly. It sounded as if he were opening a car door. He then carefully maneuvered me so I didn't hit my head on the car's roof.

Thank goodness I'd worn a pair of black slacks today instead of a miniskirt. Stepping inside a car blindfolded can't be a pretty sight, but the car had plenty of legroom. I managed somehow. Once settled, I ran my hands across the soft leather seat. If there was a silver lining in all this it was that my kidnappers appeared to be a pair of rich guys.

The smaller guy jumped in next to me, stuck his gun in my ribs and said, "Don't do anything funny, or I'll blast you."

"You'll do nothing of the kind, Ducky," the taller guy shouted from the driver's seat. "I don't want any blood splattered in my brand new car."

"I agree, Ducky," I said. "I promise to be good."

The taller guy then squealed the car's tires as we took off. I leaned back and decided to enjoy the ride. What else could I do? Besides, I needed time to figure who my kidnappers were. Their voices sounded familiar. And the cologne Ducky was wearing also smelled familiar. I'm no expert on men's fragrances, but I had smelled that cologne on someone earlier this week. But who?

And what about the short guy's nickname? Ducky? I never heard it before. Is everyone in town now giving themselves nicknames?

"How much farther, Ducky?"

"Turn right at the stop sign. Don't you remember from yesterday? It's about five minutes from here, Salty."

Salty? The tall guy driving the car was Salty. His name was on Walter Morgan's death list. Johnny and I couldn't identify him. Was the guy next to me on the list, too? If so, what was his real name? Maybe this wasn't a kidnapping after all. Maybe these guys simply wanted me to give them a manicure before the faux beauty contest began. But, why pull a gun on me?

"I hope it isn't too much farther," I said. "I need to use a restroom."

"Oh, great," the short guy replied. "I knew this would happen. Why wouldn't you let me shoot Candi in the parking lot and be done with her?"

"Shut up, Ducky," Salty said. "Stop talking like that. You're scaring me."

You think you're scared! What about me?

It took another five minutes before Salty brought the car to a stop. He jumped out of the front seat, opened the back door, and helped me out. He grabbed my arm and steered me down a path, I could hear Ducky, who was following us, mumbling to himself.

"The ground isn't very level here, so take baby steps, Miz DeCarlo, and you won't fall," Salty said. I appreciated the advice since I had worn my five-inch stilettos today. A minute later, he added, "We're coming to a series of steps. Lift your right foot. There are three of them."

Ducky unlocked a squeaky door and Salty helped me through it. Once inside, Salty asked Ducky where the restroom was.

"It's over there," Ducky said. "Are you really going to let her use it?"

"Why not?" Salty replied. "Got a better idea?"

Salty and I walked five or six steps across a room before he stopped and opened a door.

"Relax, Miz DeCarlo I'll lead you to the toilet. When you finish, shout. I'll come and get you out of here."

Once Salty left, I quickly used the toilet, but before flushing, I stood up and tried to remove my hood. I managed to lift it slightly over my right eye, enough to notice the bathroom was very plain looking. I also spotted a small window to my left. I moved closer and pulled back the yellow curtains and peeked outside. The building must be on a slight ridge. I appeared to be looking down at a body of water. Barton Lake? I was in a cabin on Barton Lake. I was still looking out the window when the door opened, and Ducky walked in.

"Just as I suspected," he shouted. "She's tried to remove the hood and is peering out the window."

Ducky grabbed my hands, tied them behind my back, and pulled me into the living room. "I told you we shouldn't trust her. She's probably figured out where we are. Let me shoot her."

"Ducky, will you please calm down. You're not shooting her. Stabbing Walter was bad enough. Besides, we don't have time. We need to get ready for the contest."

One of them grabbed me, sat me on a chair, and tied my hands to it. I guess they didn't want manicures after all.

"Where are you going?" I asked.

"None of your business," Ducky replied. "We'll be back in a few hours to get rid of you."

CHAPTER 31

After the kidnappers drove away, I leaned back in my chair. I wondered what was coming next. Ducky said they'd be back to get rid of me. That didn't sound good. If they were contestants in the faux beauty contest, I'd be safe for at least a few hours. But then, what? Ducky had a lot of pent-up anger. He just might return and shoot me. I'm too young to die. Maybe he'll win the contest and come back here in a better mood.

My stomach did a flip-flop when I remembered Salty's comment: "Stabbing Walter was enough."

These two murdered Walter Morgan on Monday night. I tried not to think about it right now.

Besides, I was more interested in wiggling out of the rope around my wrists. As I tried to work my magic, my cell phone rang to the tune of the Star-Spangled Banner. Where's my handbag? I listened more closely. My phone rang again. It was loud. My handbag was nearby. My kidnappers hadn't tied my feet. If I hopped around, maybe I could find my bag. However, as soon as I stood up, I lost my balance and fell over on my side. Ouch.

When I fell, I brushed up against an object. Maybe it was a table. For some reason, it felt like I'd been tied to a kitchen chair. In any event, I heard something plop on the tiled floor next to me. My phone rang again. The sound was louder than before. My handbag must be lying next to me.

"I'm here," I shouted a few times before realizing that it wouldn't do any good. Candi, you idiot. You need to press the talk button before anyone can hear you.

My phone rang once more, then stopped. It was probably Mandy calling from the diner. She hates being stood up.

"Is someone there?"

Oh, no, Ducky and Salty are back. They lied about being gone for a few hours.

"Please let me know if someone's there?" the voice shouted again.

Wait a minute. Ducky and Salty would never say "please." They already knew I was here. Someone was here as well, but who? I decided to find out.

"I'm here," I shouted. "Who are you?"

"Johnny Edwards. Who are you?"

"Johnny? What are you doing here?"

"Candi? Are you here to rescue me?"

"Afraid not," I said. "Two guys named Ducky and Salty kidnapped me behind Tips & Toes and drove me here."

"Oh, you mean Dougie Drake and Jane Parker."

"What? Dougie and Jane are the kidnappers?"

"Yeah, I ran into them outside Ralph's Diner on Friday night," Johnny said. "I asked Dougie if he was on Walter's death list. He went ballistic and lunged at me. Jane had to pull him off. Then, they pushed me behind the diner, threw my chair in their trunk, shoved me into their expensive-looking car, and brought me here."

"Why would Dougie go crazy about being on Walter's list?" I asked.

"I don't know," Johnny said. "I don't believe it's a death list. Charles Stewart, one of the guys on the list, told me on Thursday that everyone was a contestant in the faux queen contest."

"Did he know why Walter's name was crossed out?"

"Yeah, he said Walter had a disagreement with Dougie and didn't want anything more to do with the beauty contest."

"Did Stewart know what the disagreement was about?" I asked.

"No, he just said Walter wasn't happy about it, whatever the issue was."

"Think it may have been enough for Dougie to stab Walter?"

"It's possible. Dougie has a short fuse."

"You're right about that, Johnny, but I can't figure out what Jane Parker has to do with all of this"

"Jane must be Dougie's new girlfriend. She's in cahoots with him and helped kill Walter before trying to cover it up."

"Why do you say that?"

"One of the places on Sylvia's list was Walter's bank," Johnny said. "She must have gone there early on Tuesday morning after realizing it was open. She wanted to drop off a contest poster. Maybe Jane slipped the nail polish bottle into her purse."

"You could be right," I said. "Jane was wearing red nail polish when I ran into her on Tuesday. It wasn't the same brand we sell at the nail salon. I should have made the connection. Oh, well. Where are you, Johnny?"

"They stuck me in a bedroom closet and covered my mouth with duct tape, but I've chewed through it enough to talk," Johnny said. "They also tied my hands behind my chair. I can't wheel myself out of here and rescue you."

"Don't worry, Johnny. I'll rescue you. But first, I need to find my cell phone."

CHAPTER 32

f I could find my handbag and phone, I could call for help. I crawled around on the floor. It wasn't easy. My hands were still tied behind the chair, so I had to drag the chair along the floor with me. This was worse than exercising to those silly sunrise exercise classes I used to watch on TV.

Slowly, though, I made some progress. Within fifteen to twenty minutes, I had succeeded in moving around enough so my handbag was now directly behind my back. I tried backing up until my hands were touching it. My handbag was standing upright on the floor. That wouldn't work. I needed to tip it over, so my cell phone could fall out. I reached for one of my handbag's straps, but couldn't get a good grip on it. It was heavy. That's what I get for having too much stuff inside.

Time for Plan B. Perhaps if I kept moving around on the floor, I could stick my fingers under the bottom of the handbag and tip it over. Surely the cell phone would fall out. It was worth a try. What else could I do?

It took me another five minutes before my fingers were under my handbag. *One...two...three...push.* The handbag didn't budge. I tried again. This time, it flipped over. Great. Now, if I could find my phone lying on the floor.

While I was doing that, my cell phone rang again. I listened closely to figure out where it was on the floor. It rang a second time. I was close. I hoped whoever was calling wouldn't hang up after two rings. After the third ring. I found my phone. Now, if I could position it in my right hand, I could hit the talk button with a red acrylic nail in my left hand. The phone rang a fourth time as I hit the talk button.

"Hello, I'm here."

"Hello, is anyone there?" the caller asked.

"I'm here," I shouted. I was facing away from the phone and the caller might not hear my voice. I gently laid the phone down and tried to move around on the floor, so my head faced the phone.

"Candi, are you there? I can't hear you."

It was Mandy.

"Mandy, I'm here," I shouted at the top of my lungs.

"I can't hear you very well. What's going on?"

"I've been kidnapped," I screamed, turning around again so I didn't have to shout like a high school cheerleader.

"What? You've been kidnapped?"

"Yes, I've been kidnapped. Two men blindfolded me and tied me to a chair. I'm lying on the floor of a cabin on Barton Lake. And Johnny Edwards is here, too."

"Omigod, honey. Are the two of you okay?"

Sure, this is a great new exercise workout. I've already lost two or three pounds.

I wanted to say that, but I didn't. Instead, I asked Mandy to drive out to Barton Lake and rescue us.

"Are the kidnappers still there?"

"No, but they're coming back soon."

"I'm hanging up and calling the police. They'll send someone to save you."

"Don't go, Mandy."

Too late. She hung up. If Mandy was calling the police, maybe she'd give them my cell number. They would call in a few minutes. I needed to find my phone again and be ready to answer it this time.

"Are you still there, Candi?" I heard Johnny yelling from the bedroom closet.

"Yeah, I just talked to Mandy. She's calling the police and they're coming to rescue us."

Five minutes passed before my phone rang a third time. This time, I was ready and hit the talk button after the second ring.

"This is the Bartonsville Police Department calling," the female voice said. "Is Candi DeCarlo there?"

"I'm here, Mary," I shouted as I wiggled around on the floor.

"Are you there, Candi?"

"I'm here," I screamed.

"You don't have to shout. I may be old, but I haven't lost my hearing yet. What's your problem anyway?"

"Didn't Mandy tell you? I've been kidnapped. I'm lying on the floor of a cabin at Barton Lake."

"She told me, but I'm having a hard time believing it. Sure, you're not pulling my leg? Maybe you and Mandy had one too many at the Hideaway tonight, and thought it'd be fun to call and play a trick on me."

"Mary, I'm forty-two. I'm a professional manicurist. A grandmother of two. I'm not playing games with you. I've been kidnapped and so has Johnny Edwards."

"Why was Johnny kidnapped?" Mary said. "Put him on the phone."

"I can't. He's locked in a closet."

"Never figured him that way." Mary said. "Okay, exactly what cabin are you in on Barton Lake?"

"Tell her it belongs to Dougie," Johnny shouted.

"I heard him," Mary said. "Okay, Candi. Let me find Chief Cobb and tell him what's happened to you and Johnny."

"Don't hang up, Mary. I can't keep wiggling around on the floor to answer my phone."

"Hang on. I'll call him on my other line."

Mary came back on the line two or three minutes later.

"I've told Chief Cobb what's happened. He's on his way, but first he needs to find out how to get there and which cabin belongs to Dougie. He's never been to Barton Lake before."

"Have him contact Nate, or Sheriff Pickle," Johnny shouted. "They'll know."

"Will do," Mary said. "In the meantime, how did you know Dougie kidnapped you?"

"His cologne gave him away, and maybe his nickname, now that I think of it."

"What are you talking about?"

"The taller guy who Johnny says is Jane Parker called him Ducky. Doesn't Dougie's last name have something to do with ducks?"

"Sure," Mary said. "A male duck is called a drake."

They put a hood over my head, but they didn't do that to Johnny."

"Damn," Mary said before picking up another caller.

CHAPTER 33

About ten minutes later, I heard a car pull into the driveway in front of Dougie's cabin.

"Are you still there, Mary?" I shouted into my cell phone.

"Yep, I'm still here. Chief Cobb just radioed me. He's at the cabin. You can relax now."

What a relief. I was glad Dan arrived before Dougie and Jane came back from the faux beauty contest. A minute later, Dan walked through the front door and spotted me lying on the kitchen floor.

"Are you okay, Candi?" he asked. I could feel him bending down and carefully removing the hood covering my head.

"Thanks, Dan," I said after the hood came off and I was staring up into his beautiful big brown eyes.

"No problem," he said, smiling at me. "Let me untie your arms."

When he finished, Dan helped me to my feet. He then picked up my cell phone and handed it to me.

"Mary, thanks for believing my story," I said. "Dan is here, and he's rescued me."

"I'm glad you're okay, Candi. Now, let me speak to him."

I handed the phone to Dan. While they talked, I went looking for Johnny. I found him in a tiny bedroom off the kitchen.

"Johnny, it's me, Candi," I said, slowly opening the closet door. "Close your eyes. It's bright in this room. You may have trouble adjusting your eyes to the light."

"Don't worry," Johnny replied. "You'll be a sight for sore eyes."

When we entered the kitchen a minute later, Dan handed me back my phone and said, "Let's go."

"Where are we going?"

"Back to town," he said, "Mary says one of my guys spotted Dougie and Jane walking across the town square twenty minutes ago. They were carrying duffle bags and garment bags over their shoulders."

Dan and I placed Johnny's wheelchair in the police van and then helped him into the back seat before we took off.

"Did Mary tell you what Dougie and Jane were wearing?" I asked.

"Mary didn't say but let me call her and find out. Why are you asking?"

"Dougie and Jane had on expensive-looking blue sweatsuits."

Dan picked up his car radio and called Mary. She didn't know about the sweatsuits, but promised to check with the officer who spotted them. While we waited, Dan asked why I thought Dougie was one of the kidnappers.

"That's easy," I said. "Dougie and Jane grabbed Johnny on Friday night in front of Ralph's Diner. They were wearing matching sweatsuits when they approached my truck Saturday afternoon, but they were wearing ski masks. I had no idea who they were until Johnny and I discovered each other at the cabin, and he told me about his kidnapping."

"Why did they kidnap you?"

"They didn't say too much in front of me," I said, "but my guess is they murdered Walter."

"Why do you say that?"

"Dougie wanted to shoot me in the parking lot behind Tips & Toes. That's when Salty or Jane told him he couldn't kill me. Walter's death had been enough."

"That's interesting," Dan said. "It may help explain why the town president acted so peculiar all week."

"What do you mean?"

"A day or two after Walter's murder, he walked into my office. He wanted to know if I had considered Juan Hernandez as a possible murder suspect. When I said 'no,' the town president said I should look at him. A bank teller told him that

Walter Morgan recently rejected Juan's request for a bank loan to expand his office cleaning business."

"Was that bank teller Marlene Murphy?" Johnny asked.

"The town president didn't say. Why are you asking?"

"Marlene is dating Dougie's younger brother," Johnny said.

"I never thought of a connection like that," Dan said.

"You're still new in town," I said. "You wouldn't know about Marlene and Dougie's brother."

"I want to know one thing, Johnny." Dan said. "How do you know about every relationship in Bartonsville?"

"I wheel around town all day. Nobody pays any attention to me, but I notice things."

"Did you bring Juan in for questioning?" I asked.

"Juan doesn't speak English very well," Dan said. "At first, we had a difficult time understanding him. His story about a cousin in Mexico ultimately loaning him money after Walter turned him down seemed far-fetched. But as I was set to let him go, the prosecutor called me the next morning. Told me to arrest Juan. He had enough evidence to take him to trial and get a conviction."

"That sounds like Darrell Sheridan," I said. "He loves locking up people whether they're guilty or not. And you probably didn't know this, either. He and Dougie were college roommates."

"Is everybody in this town related to everyone else?" Dan asked.

"It's why if you don't know the right people, you're toast," Johnny said.

"I've got a question for you, Dan," I said.

"What's that?"

"When I told you the other day that Sylvia hadn't met Walter on Monday night, you claimed that you had found some incriminating evidence on Walter's desk."

"Let me guess what it was," Johnny piped up.

Dan smiled. "Okay, let's hear your theory."

"Candi asked me to track down the contestants for the faux beauty contest," Johnny said. "One of them, Charles Stewart, sits on the Youth Center board. He told me the board members were concerned that someone was embezzling money from the Center."

"Did they suspect Sylvia?" I asked.

"No, Stewart said the board members thought it was Dougie. He likes to gamble at the riverboat casinos, but he isn't very lucky."

"Maybe Walter was planning to expose Dougie. When Dougie found out, he panicked and stabbed Walter with Jane's help," Johnny said.

"Very good," Dan said. "Maybe I should hire the two of you as investigators."

"I'm available," Johnny said.

"I've got another question, Dan," I said.

"What?"

"Why did Dougie and Jane paint Walter's nails pink?"

"Haven't you figured that out yet, Candi?"

"No."

"I'm surprised you don't have a theory. It was probably Jane's idea. She must have known you were taking care of Walter's hangnails. She painted his nails, so it would look like you were in his office and stabbed Walter."

"I bet they left the information about the Drake Center on Walter's desk, so it would look like Sylvia was embezzling the money." Johnny said.

"Like I said, maybe I should hire the two of you as investigators."

We finally made it back to town. Dan found a parking spot behind Ralph's Diner. As we walked around the corner, hundreds of people were milling about on the town square.

"What are we going to do now?" I asked.

"I need to see if my guys found Douglas and Jane," Dan said, picking up his mobile radio. "You two should probably stay here, out of the way. If Douglas still has his gun, he might take a pot shot at both of you."

CHAPTER 34

After Dan spoke to someone on his mobile radio, he took off towards Pete's Bar. Pete makes a mean margarita. Maybe Dougie and Jane dropped by there for a quick drink before the faux beauty contest began and forgot to leave. I hoped so. I already had enough excitement for one day.

"Should we stay here like the Chief told us?" Johnny asked.

"No way," I replied. "I need to find Mandy. She's probably worried sick about what's happened to me. We're like sisters. We know what each of us is doing all the time. You're welcome to come with me."

I glanced at my Betty Boop watch. It was almost eight o'clock. Knowing Mandy, it was possible that she grew tired of waiting and drove home to enjoy her nightly bubble bath. I called her house first. No answer. Next call was to her cell.

"Where are you?" Mandy screeched after picking up her phone.

"I'm in front of the diner. Where are you?"

"Next to Tips & Toes. Are you okay? I've been worried sick about you."

I assured Mandy that Johnny and I were both fine before telling her how Dan found us tied up inside Dougie's cabin at Barton Lake and drove us back to town.

"I'm so glad you're safe. Stay where you are. I'll be right there."

I tossed the phone in my handbag and waited. A minute later, I spotted Mandy running down the sidewalk with her arms open wide.

Who knew she could run?

Mandy gave me a huge, sweaty hug before bending down and squeezing Johnny's hand.

He had a big smile on his face.

"I can't believe Dougie kidnapped the two of you," Mandy said. "What's up with that?"

"We think it had something to do with Walter Morgan's murder," I said.

"Dougie murdered Walter?"

"We're convinced that he did," Johnny said. "But Chief Cobb is still looking for some more answers from him."

"Want to watch the faux beauty contest?" I asked, changing the subject. "It's starting in a few minutes."

"Why not?" Mandy said, finally removing her left arm from around my shoulder. "What else could happen tonight?"

The three of us walked a half block to where the stage for the Foliage Festival Queen contest had been set up. A large crowd was milling about anxiously waiting for the contest to begin.

A minute later, Martha Rae Folger, the contest emcee, strode across the stage.

"Good evening, ladies and gentlemen," she said into a wireless microphone. "Welcome to the annual Barton County Foliage Festival Queen competition. We have a great group of ladies competing for this year's title, so without further ado, let's bring them out."

The curtain opened behind Martha Rae and out came this year's competitors, all dressed in evening gowns.

"What's going on?" Mandy asked. She was first to notice that there were two types of competitors. "Why are those old guys dressed in drag?"

"They're the faux beauty contestants," I replied.

Four men were strutting around the stage, waving and blowing air kisses at the crowd and generally acting obnoxious.

"Okay, ladies and gentlemen," Martha Rae said. "As you can see, we have some older competitors this year. They're here to help raise money for the Drayton Drake Youth Center. Let me ask our younger contestants to step backstage for a few minutes. I need all of you to vote now for your favorite older Queen. Place your dollar bills in the baskets in front of each of them. Whoever raises the most money wins the faux beauty contest."

The drag queens stopped strutting and stood in front of their baskets as the crowd pressed forward with money in their hands.

"This is disgusting?" Mandy said as she shook her head. "These guys should be ashamed of themselves."

"Honey, don't be so upset," I said. "They're doing it for charity. If they can raise enough money, Sylvia says the Youth Center can reopen before Christmas."

"I guess it's okay then," Mandy said, dropping some dollar bills in the basket in front of the guy in a red dress.

"I bet I'd look good in that dress," Mandy said. "I wonder where he bought it. Enough about that. Who are these guys, anyway?"

"I recognize one of them even with his blonde wig and smoky eyes," I said, pointing at the shortest contestant on stage. "It's Dougie Drake in that turquoise sequined gown."

"You're right, Candi," Johnny said. "And the one in the red dress is Jane Parker. What's she doing in the contest?"

"She isn't the most attractive woman I've ever met," Mandy said. "Maybe, this is the only type of beauty contest she could enter."

Should we find Chief Cobb and let him know?" Johnny asked.

"Dan could be anywhere," I replied. "Let me call the police station and ask Mary to track him down."

"I've got a better idea," Johnny said. He spun around in his chair and headed for the handicap ramp at the side of the stage. He kept yelling at people to get out of his way.

Johnny was making his way to the stage when Dougie spotted him. Dougie let out a loud gasp and jumped off the stage, rolling over on the lawn a few times before he stood up and began running away. Dougie didn't get very far at first, but soon realized that if he kicked off his high heels and hitched up his gown, he could run faster.

"Let's go," I said to Mandy.

"Where are we going?"

"We're chasing after Dougie, but maybe I should make a call first," I said, grabbing my cell phone out of my handbag.

"Good evening, Bartonsville Police Department. How can we help you?"

"Mary, it's Candi. Where's Dan?"

"What's up now?"

"Dougie jumped off the stage in his turquoise sequined gown and is running away."

"Good Lord, I hope you catch him and grab a photo. I'd love to see it. What direction is he headed so I can tell the Chief?"

I told Mary that Dougie was running towards the alley behind Ralph's Diner before grabbing Mandy by the arm.

"Not so fast, Candi," Mandy screamed. "I'm already sweaty. My makeup is running."

"Okay, I'll go ahead, and you can catch up."

Dougie was about fifteen feet in front of me, but as he jogged into the alley, I shortened the distance between us.

"Stop, Dougie!" I yelled. "You can't run away. You'll be caught sooner or later."

"Shut up, Candi. You forgot that I ran track in high school."

"Huh?"

Dougie never ran track. He was in the Drama Club. And he was pretty bad at it. He was always forgetting his lines and singing off-key.

I was now within ten feet of him. Dougie looked around to see where I was and fell against the diner's dumpster. It slowed him down enough that I managed to tackle him to the ground.

"Get off me, Candi!" he yelped. "You're heavy and you're hurting me."

"Heavy, huh," I said, slamming my body down on Dougie's chest. "I'll show you heavy."

"That's enough, Candi," Dan said as he and Nate Sloan pulled me off Dougie and helped me to my feet. Nate then knelt and placed a pair of handcuffs on Dougie, who was still wiggling like a goldfish that had jumped out of its bowl.

"Let me hit him again," I said, mad as hell that Dougie called me fat.

"Candi, if you hit him again, Dougie's likely to file assault charges against you," Mandy said. She had finally caught up to me and was trying to catch her breath.

"Thanks, Miz Malone," Dan said. "I'm sure Candi appreciates your legal advice."

"Hold on!" we heard a voice behind us shout. "Let me get a picture of this."

J. Michael McPherson was jogging down the alley with his camera.

"I need a picture for tomorrow's paper," he said. "Give me a second to catch my breath and set up my camera."

As McPherson fumbled with his camera, I noticed Mandy was now standing next to Dan and Dougie.

What's up with that?

"Okay, I'm ready," McPherson announced. "Everyone say 'cheese!'"

Dan grabbed Dougie by the arm and steered him towards his police cruiser.

"Can I ask you a question, Candi?" Nate asked.

"Sure thing."

"Where did you learn to tackle like that?"

"Bobby. He made me sit next to him on Sunday afternoons and watch NFL games."

"Too bad you're a woman," Nate replied. "The Indianapolis Colts could use a good tackler."

CHAPTER 35

It was nearing eleven o'clock on Sunday morning when I rolled over in bed and glanced at my alarm clock. I couldn't believe I'd slept so long. All the excitement of the past week had finally caught up to me.

I crawled out of bed, grabbed a quick shower, and threw on a pair of jeans and an old Brigadiers sweatshirt. I usually spend Sunday afternoons cleaning my apartment or doing laundry at Sun & Suds. Today was no different. I had a ton of clothes to clean, thanks to whomever broke into my apartment on Thursday night and scattered them all over the place. I needed to wash everything the intruder's dirty hands had touched. I was now convinced it was Dougie Drake.

I was also starving. I hadn't eaten since Saturday afternoon. Dougie and Jane hadn't been the greatest hosts.

I hauled my laundry basket down my apartment stairs, lifted it into my truck, and headed for the laundromat. But first, I needed to stop by the Grab & Run. On weekends, they serve biscuits and gravy.

Sanjay "Sonny" Patel, the store's owner, was standing behind the counter reading the Sunday edition of the *Barton County Beacon.* He's a short, dark-haired man with an electric smile and a positive outlook on life.

"Good morning, young lady," Sonny said.

I love Sonny.

"What you need, Candi?"

"Give me a full order of biscuits and gravy today."

"Must be hungry. I get busy and fix biscuits for you."

As he worked away at the rear counter, Sonny turned slightly and asked, "Did you hear about the town president? Bad man. Caught last night in dress. Picture in paper today."

"I heard something about it, but haven't seen any pictures yet. Can I look at your paper?"

I picked up Sonny's paper off the front counter. There it was: a full-color photograph of Dougie in his turquoise sequined gown along with Dan and Mandy standing on either side of him.

"You know lady in photo?" Sonny asked as he handed me a large Styrofoam container of biscuits and gravy.

"Yes, she's my best friend and a picture hog."

"I remember her now," Sonny said. "Tire lady. I went to her store to buy tires for my SUV. She names price. I say how about discount. 'You come to my store; I give you discount.' She says, 'No way, Jose.' I say, 'My name isn't Jose, it's Sonny.'"

"That sounds like Mandy," I said. "She probably wouldn't give me a discount either. How much do I owe you, Sonny?"

"Free today, young lady. In good mood. Even give you my paper."

I threw Sonny an air kiss and left his store. Next stop was the laundromat. It was empty when I entered so I broke their rule and tossed my clothes in three washers instead of the two you are normally allowed to use at one time.

As I sat down to enjoy my biscuits and gravy, I pulled out Sonny's paper and began reading McPherson's front-page story.

He made it sound like Mandy, and not me, had captured Dougie last night. There goes my football career. Oh, well.

"Reading about Dougie?" a male voice said.

I looked up. Nate Sloan was holding a pillowcase full of dirty clothes.

"What are you doing here?" I asked. "Doesn't your mother do your laundry?"

"No," Nate replied. "She makes me do my own. Ever since I was a teenager. I usually do it at home, but Mom spent the entire morning whining about her business plans. I was tired of listening to her, so I came here."

"Is she still mad at Madge for kicking her out of the salon?"

"Yeah, she says Madge is a silly old woman who is out of touch with what consumers want to buy these days. She intends to rent space from another merchant on the town square. If that doesn't work out, she'll open her own shop in one of the empty storefronts. Mom is determined to show up Madge."

"I wish her luck," I said. "I never thought cosmetics, aromatherapy candles, and nails went together very well."

"How come McPherson took a picture of Mandy and not you?" Nate asked.

"That's a good question," I replied. "Mandy jumped in front of me before I figured out what she was doing."

"Mandy must have thought it'd help her tire business if she was seen as the one who captured Dougie," Nate said.

"I guess so." I replied. "So, what's going to happen to him and Jane now?"

"They'll appear before Judge Stone tomorrow morning and be formally charged. Chief Cobb still hadn't talked with the prosecutor last night when I left work, but my guess is Dougie and Jane will both be charged with murder. But their troubles won't end there."

"What do you mean?"

"Chief Cobb also talked to someone from the Indy office of the FBI last night. They're sending an agent here tomorrow to discuss charging Dougie and Jane with kidnapping you and Johnny."

"Wow," I said. "When did you guys catch Jane?"

"Early this morning. Chief Cobb sent two officers to her house. They nabbed her as she was throwing clothes into a suitcase and preparing to leave town."

"Who's going to run the bank now that Walter is dead, and Jane is in jail?" I said. "I hope there's not a run on the place. I'd hate to lose what little money I have in my savings account."

"I hope it doesn't happen either, but who knows," Nate said. "Listen, Candi, I just realized I forgot to bring some laundry soap with me. Can I borrow some from you?"

"Sure thing," I said. "Let's wash this whole event down the drain."

CHAPTER 36

"Well, if it isn't our local hero," Joanie said as I walked into Ralph's Diner on Tuesday morning. "Want your usual?"

"Yes," I said, sitting down at the lunch counter. "What's going on?"

"You tell me, hero," Joanie said as she handed me a cinnamon swirl and medium Diet Dr. Pepper.

"I spent my day off picking up the donation jars for Sylvia Wilson's legal defense fund. I then dropped by Sylvia's place and handed her the money. We collected nearly a thousand dollars."

"Wow, that's great," Joanie replied. "What's she going to do with it?"

"Sylvia said the Youth Center only raised a few hundred dollars at the faux beauty contest. It would have been more if Dougie hadn't jumped off the stage and run away. The legal defense funds will be used to finish the Center's renovations."

"That's nice, Candi," Joanie said. "Does it make you feel good?"

"Yup."

"Well, look who's here," Joanie said.

I spun around on my stool. Johnny Edwards was carefully steering his motorized wheelchair around some tables and chairs to reach the lunch counter.

"What's with the big smile?" I asked.

"I got a job yesterday," he said.

"Did Dan hire you as an investigator?"

"No, I wish. Martha Rae took me back. Said I deserved a second chance. She's even going to pay me more than she did before."

"That's terrific," I said, reaching over and giving Johnny a hug. "Congratulations. When do you start?"

"I'm already on the job," he said. "Look, Martha Rae handed me this tiny portable recorder, so I don't misquote anyone again."

"Is that thing on right now?"

"No, I'll let you know when I want to quote you. Listen, I've got to run. I'm already working on a story."

Once Johnny left, Joanie leaned on the counter.

"He seems so happy," she said. "Maybe he'll give McPherson a run for his money. Fatso could use some competition."

"Fatso? You're calling him that now because he never tips you."

"How can I retire if McPherson won't leave me a few nickels and dimes," Joanie said. "It's not like he spends his money on clothes."

I laughed. "Listen, I need to go, too. I don't want to start the week being late for work."

"Good morning, Madge," I said after entering Tips 'n Toes a few minutes later.

"Our town's newest hero," she said, flashing me a huge smile.

"Why did you say that?"

"I talked to Johnny Edwards. He told me what happened at the Foliage Festival on Saturday night. How you tackled Dougie Drake as he tried to escape in an evening gown. What was up with that?"

I gave Madge a quick summary of the events, including how Dougie and Jane Parker kidnapped me earlier on Saturday night.

"Oh, my goodness, honey, you must have been frightened out of your mind." Madge said when I finished.

"It was scary until Dan rescued me and Johnny, who was also kidnapped," I said. "Dougie kept waving a gun in my face and threatening to shoot me."

"I'm glad you're safe and ready to get to work."

"Can I ask you a question, Madge?"

"Sure."

"Did Johnny say he wanted to quote you?"

"Yeah, he had this tiny recorder. He played back my quotes. They sounded good. He said it'll be on WYMN later today or tomorrow."

Darn him. He's become as bad as McPherson.

An hour into the day, I looked up and noticed Irene Morgan had entered the nail salon. What's she doing here? She momentarily spoke to Madge before walking back to my station.

"Good morning, Irene," I said, smiling at her.

"I'd like a manicure," she said. "I've never had one before. Can I sit down?"

"Absolutely," I said, helping her into my chair. "Let me take a look at your nails."

After showing Irene a chart with different nail choices, she decided on French nails.

"Good choice," I said. "They'll make you look very sophisticated. By the way, what's happening at the bank?"

"I've decided to take over as the bank president."

"You did?"

"Yes, I know what you're thinking. What does she know about running a bank? A lot, actually. In addition to listening to Walter's endless chatter about his work for years, I was raised in a banking family. My father once owned his own state bank."

"Well, I'm sure you'll do a fine job," I said.

"I've also persuaded Louise Dorfman to become my assistant. She's taking over Jane Parker's responsibilities."

"Louise is a wonderful person," I said. "She'll be a great help to you. Well, what do you think of your French nails?"

"They're beautiful," Irene said, handing me a twenty-dollar tip. "When do I need to come back again?"

"In four or five weeks," I said. "Madge will set you up with an appointment."

I had another client right after Irene left. I didn't have a chance to ask Madge if Irene scheduled another appointment. When Madge finally wandered back to my nail station a few hours later, she motioned for me to follow her into the storage room.

"Is something wrong, Madge?" I asked.

"No," she said, closing the door behind her. "I wanted to tell you about my conversation with Irene Morgan."

"Was she okay with her French nails?"

"She was ecstatic. Irene thought they were gorgeous. Said you were a magician. She should have had her nails done years ago."

"I'm glad she liked them," I replied. "Irene deserves some happiness in her life."

"Irene also told me of the changes she's going to make at the bank. She will send all her female bank tellers to us for French nails. Irene said the nails will complement the new uniforms she has ordered for them."

"Wow, sounds like Irene plans to shake things up at the bank."

"It does, but that's not the real reason I wanted to talk with you," Madge said. "You have been doing a good job lately. It's time to give you a raise. There will be an extra twenty-five dollars in your paycheck this week."

"Thanks, Madge," I said. "That's quite a surprise."

"Don't tell Trudy," Madge said as she left the storage room. "I don't want her to quit in a huff."

The rest of the day was uneventful. Madge let me and Trudy leave early. No doubt she and her girlfriends were headed to a riverboat casino. I stopped by the Grab & Run on my way home to fill up my truck with gas and buy two pieces of their broasted chicken.

I ate my chicken, then called Mandy to see what was happening with her. We hadn't talked since Saturday night.

Mandy answered on the second ring.

"Howdy, girlfriend," she said. "What's up?"

"Lots," I said before telling Mandy about my day. I mentioned how Johnny was working again at WYMN. I also told her that Irene Morgan ordered French nails for herself and she was taking over as president of the bank. And, finally, how Madge gave me a raise.

"Whew, you had quite a busy day," Mandy said when I finished. "The past forty-eight hours have been busy for me, too."

"How so?"

"Business has been crazy," Mandy said. "Folks kept dropping by to congratulate me on capturing Dougie Drake. McPherson's story in Sunday's paper and his photo of me and Chief Cobb with Dougie has been very helpful. I couldn't buy that kind of publicity."

Glad I could tackle Dougie for you. I felt like saying that, but why deflate Mandy's balloon? She hadn't sounded so positive in a long time.

"I've also been appointed to the town council," Mandy said.

"What?"

"Yeah, George Pardee called me on Monday morning. Said he was becoming the new town president now that Dougie is in jail. He asked me to fill out the remainder of Dougie's term on the town council. Said he'd been a close friend of my late husband and it was time to have a woman on the council."

"Is that all it took?"

"No, he had to convene the Republican caucus last night. He told the party faithful of his plans and they all voted in favor of my appointment."

"By the way, when did you become a Republican?"

"Yesterday."

Why am I not surprised.

CANDI DECARLO MYSTERY BOOK 2

NAIL BITER

THE MYSTERY OF THE CLOBBERED COACH

My best friend, Mandy Malone, always parks her shiny black Jaguar convertible behind Ralph's Diner. That way, she says, it's less likely to get scratched by some careless local yokel.

"What's the game plan tonight?" I asked her, after we buckled up and took off for the high school football field.

"See those flyers in the back seat?" Mandy said, tilting her head slightly in that direction. "There's five thousand of them. I picked them up earlier today at the UPS store. We're going to pass out as many as we can tonight."

Wow. Did Mandy think that half the town would be at tonight's season-opening football game?

"Is the football game the best place to pass them out?" I asked.

"It's like this," Mandy said. "I have an opponent in my upcoming election. The political consultant I hired last week says I need to be seen around town, pressing the flesh whenever I can."

"So, that's why you dragged me out tonight?"

Mandy forced a tiny smile. "Actually, I want the boys' parents to see me and think I care about their pimply-faced sons."

"Your opponent, Dottie Rosenblatt, told me all about your election on Tuesday."

"Wait a minute. You've met my opponent?" Mandy said, slamming her brakes in the middle of the road. "Quick, tell me all about her."

"Don't get so excited," I replied. "Dottie's a regular of mine. She drops by Tips & Toes every four or five weeks unless she has a nail emergency."

"Who is she and why is she running against me?"

"Dottie's a widow who works as a nurse at the high school. I don't know why she's running against you. I didn't ask her."

"George Pardee!" Mandy shouted as she eased up on her brake. "He's probably behind it. As the new town president, he hates it when I don't vote with him and the other good old boys on the town council. So, he's found this babe to run against me."

"Wait a minute. Isn't George Pardee a Republican like you?" I asked. "Dottie's a Democrat. All I know is she's awfully nice, and she's a good tipper, too."

"Candi, do me a favor?"

"What?"

"Next time, she shows up, ask her a bunch of questions. See if you can drudge up some dirt on her and pass it along to me."

Dig up your own dirt.

As we approached the football field, the adjacent parking lot looked full. "Where should we park?" I asked.

"Don't worry," Mandy replied. "I've already taken care of that."

"What do you mean?"

"I called the police station this afternoon and found out that Nate Sloan had traffic duty tonight. He promised to save me a space."

Poor Nate. He still hasn't overcome his high school crush on Mandy. He's probably not alone. Most of the boys followed her around the school like little puppy dogs. Unfortunately, Nate was extremely shy, and never worked up the courage to ask her out. Not that it would have mattered. Mandy was only interested in bad boys. It's how she ended up marrying her first husband, a badass biker named Butch Muldoon.

Nate directed us to a prime spot just inside the entrance to the parking lot. Mandy and I then grabbed some flyers from her back seat.

"You can position yourself next to the concession stand," Mandy said. "I'll wander into the stands and pass out my flyers."

That sounded fine to me. I was dead tired from attaching blue and white streamers to the salon's ceiling all day. My boss, Madge Parsons, wanted everyone to know we were full of school spirit. Standing still would be a piece of cake.

It didn't turn out that way, however. Nobody cared about Mandy's flyer. I needed to pass them out before people reached the concession stand. Once they bought their hot dogs, popcorn, pretzel and soft drinks, they didn't have an empty hand for a flyer.

Most people were polite enough and took one. But I later noticed that they either tossed the flyer on the ground or threw it in the garbage can next to the concession stand.

At halftime, I looked up and spotted Lonnie Sparks making her way to the concession stand. She's one of my regulars.

"What are you doing here, Candi?" she asked.

"Helping Mandy pass out campaign flyers."

Lonnie grabbed a flyer and studied it closely for a minute before handing it back. "I hope Mandy won't be as tight with the town's money as she is at her discount tire store. I bought a new set of tires from her recently. She wouldn't give me a senior discount even though I have the AAA and AARP discount cards."

"I'll mention it to her," I said. "Seniors on fixed incomes deserve a break."

"Darn right we do, but it's not a problem for me. Thankfully, my late husband, Jimmy, left me plenty of money before he passed away."

Lonnie appeared to be tearing up, so I quickly changed the subject.

"Thanks for posting your latest blue-and-white striped nails on Facebook last night," I said. "Your friends showed up this morning and all wanted their nails done like yours."

"What can I say, I'm a trendsetter," Lonnie replied, glancing down at her nails. "Maybe I should run for public office like your friend. I wouldn't be afraid to spend the town's money."

"I'd vote for you," I said. "And, by the way, you look stunning in your new blue-and-white striped dress."

"Thanks, Candi," Lonnie said. "That's sweet of you to notice. Now, if you'll excuse me, I need to grab an Italian sausage with onions and sweet peppers and a large Mountain Dew before the second half begins."

Once play resumed, the area around the concession stand was like a ghost town. I thought about looking for Mandy in the stands, but I was too tired to move. Instead, I bought myself a Diet Dr. Pepper and sat down at a nearby picnic table. The score must be close. I kept hearing loud cheers from the stands. Maybe the Bartonsville Brigadiers under their legendary coach Charlie "Stubby" Watson had a real chance to win.

Nearly ten minutes had past when I noticed Mandy charging towards me.

"What are you doing? Why aren't you passing out flyers?"

"See any people?" I replied. "Everybody is in the stands watching the game."

"Oh," Mandy said, after glancing around. "I guess you're right."

"How did you make out?"

"Some people were nice, took a flyer and stuffed it in their back pockets, but most were downright rude," Mandy said. "One woman accused me of taking her away from the game. She stood up and seemed ready to punch me."

"So much for promoting democracy among the masses," I said. "I'm thinking this wasn't a good idea. This crowd isn't interested in politics. I doubt if any of them can even name a single member of the town council."

"You're probably right, Candi. They'll end up getting the candidates they deserve."

"Don't put yourself in that category," I said. "You're better than that, however, I did receive one complaint about you tonight."

"Who was it?"

"Lonnie Sparks. You didn't offer her a senior discount when she recently bought some tires from you."

"Lonnie has more money than she knows how to spend it," Mandy said. "But maybe she has a point. My political consultant says it's a proven fact that seniors vote, and dumb high school football fans don't. Maybe I should start offering senior discounts."

"Are we finished for the night?"

"No," Mandy said. "Let me buy you a drink before we call it a night?"

I didn't feel like a drink. I was dead tired, and already knew that tomorrow would be a busy day at the salon. However, I didn't want to disappoint my best friend. She seemed down in the dumps, so I agreed.

Mandy flipped on the town's radio station, WYMN-FM, to check the football game score as we drove to Rick's Hideaway Lounge. Phil and Bill, the Jensen twins, have broadcast Brigadier football games for twenty plus years.

"Let's play a game," Mandy said, turning up the volume on her radio. "Let's see how long it takes the Jensens to announce the score. They usually start chatting about themselves or some former player they met before the game and forget why they're really there."

"You're on," I said setting the stopwatch function on my Betty Boop watch.

It took us another five minutes before we reached Rick's Hideaway Lounge on the east side of town. The place was empty except for a few regulars sitting at the bar sipping their beers.

"Well, look who just brightened my day," Rick Ives said as we sat down on a pair of bar stools. Rick is a still handsome sixtyish year old man with dark hair and silver streaks running through it. He owns the bar. "What can I get my two favorite ladies?"

"You're such a sweet talker, Rick, but save your breath," Mandy said. "Bring us two strawberry daiquiris."

Rick bowed to her and started making our drinks.

"What brings you ladies out tonight?" he asked after delivering the drinks a few minutes later.

"We've been campaigning," Mandy said. "I'm running for town council."

"Good for you," he replied. "I seem to remember hearing something about how you were appointed after Dougie Drake went to prison for murdering Walter Morgan. Good luck. I'll vote for you."

"Thanks, Rick," Mandy said. "Say, any chance I can leave some flyers for your customers."

"Sorry, can't help you there," Rick said. "If I let you pass out your stuff, your opponents will want me to do the same thing for them. Pretty soon, little old ladies who sell Tupperware products will be after me. However, you can do anything you want in my parking lot."

Rick walked away to wait on another customer. I suggested to Mandy that we wait until people showed up after the game ended and leave flyers under their windshield wipers.

"Won't they be the same idiots who didn't take my flyer at the game?"

"Yeah," I replied, "But they'll be more likely to toss the flyer on their front seats before they drive home. It will give them an alibi if the cops pull them over."

"Good idea," Mandy said before taking a long swig of her drink.

We didn't have to wait long. Dozens of folks began pouring into Rick's. We asked a few about the final score. True to form, the Jansens hadn't mentioned it on our way to Rick's. Turns out the Brigadiers lost by a field goal. While most folks were disappointed, they thought the team played better than they did last season.

Mandy and I sat at the bar another ten minutes before finishing our drinks and slipping into the parking lot. We grabbed some flyers from Mandy's car and began sticking them on the parked cars. We decided to work together in case some weirdo might be lurking in the shadows.

Mandy and I had covered most of the vehicles when I heard a loud noise that sounded like a gunshot.

"Did you hear that?" I asked.

"Yeah, it came from over there," Mandy said, pointing to her left.

"Let's check it out."

As we walked towards the sound, we noticed a four-door sedan parked by itself. The passenger side window was smashed in, and the driver was slumped over his steering wheel.

"Omigod!" I screamed. "It's Coach Watson!"

COMING SOON!

Be sure to pick up a copy at your
favorite local independent bookstore or from an online retailer.

ACKNOWLEDGEMENTS

Members of my critique group, *In Mysterious Company*, deserves much of the credit for this book's existence. Over the years, they regularly met, read and offered critiques on my short stories, especially those featuring Candi DeCarlo.

These published writers need to be recognized publicly for all their help. They include Diana Catt, Michael Dabney, Michael Eldridge, Marianne Halbert, Shari Held, Brigitte Kephart and Janet Williams. It has been an absolute pleasure working with them.

I would be remiss if I also didn't mention the late S.M. Harding. She started our group and was definitely one of my biggest "critics" when reviewing my work, but I learned so much from her. I still miss her presence at our meetings.

Thanks to my wife, Rebecca Reddick, who allowed me to work on my stories when I should have been doing my share of the household chores.

Finally, special thanks to Robin Surface, publisher of Fideli Publishing, for working with me on this novel and a recent nonfiction book I wrote about the Indiana state flag. Robin, you are the best!

Any shortcomings you find with this novel are my fault, so don't blame the folks mentioned above. Thank you.